"A trap!" t
clawing f

He never had a chance to draw it, as a burst of gunfire ripped through the door and caught him in the side. McCarter leaped across the coffee table, breaking for the window, wondering, briefly, if Bolan's arm of the mission had been compromised, as well.

The Phoenix Force fighter wrapped his arms around his head and launched himself through the glass, continuing on down the fire escape in a jolting ride that left him bruised and aching—but alive.

He raced down the narrow alley and was almost to the street when a car turned in ahead of him, headlights blazing. McCarter heard the doors open and sensed the weapons leveled at him. Footsteps sounded on the pavement behind him.

"Your move," he told the men surrounding him as he raised his hands.

A gun butt slammed against the back of his skull and fireworks detonated in his head, the bright sparks fading instantly to black.

MACK BOLAN®

The Executioner

DON PENDLETON'S
THE EXECUTIONER®
FEATURING MACK BOLAN®
BLOOD RULES

A GOLD EAGLE BOOK FROM
WORLDWIDE®

TORONTO • NEW YORK • LONDON • PARIS
AMSTERDAM • STOCKHOLM • HAMBURG
ATHENS • MILAN • TOKYO • SYDNEY

First edition May 1991

ISBN 0-373-61149-8

Special thanks and acknowledgment to
Mike Newton for his contribution to this work.

BLOOD RULES

The last pleasure in life is the sense of discharging our duty.

—William Hazlitt

In comradeship is danger encountered best.
—Goethe

I have my closest comrades with me in this time of danger, and if discharging our duty becomes the last act of our lives, so be it. We recognize the enemy, and he has dues to pay.

—Mack Bolan

To the men and women who work so valiantly
in the war against drugs.
God keep.

PROLOGUE

Bogotá, Colombia

The bodyguards had once embarrassed Julio Gallon until he came to understand that they were necessary for survival on the streets of Bogotá. Each morning when he kissed his wife goodbye two men were waiting on his doorstep, weapons bulging underneath their coats. They followed him around all day, remaining in the courtroom while he did his job and trailing him to lunch like watchdogs, constantly alert for enemies. When he was finished working, they saw him home and were relieved by others who remained on guard throughout the night, a thin line of defense between his family and the men who wished to see him dead.

Of course, it would be nothing personal if he was killed. Gallon had been a judge in Bogotá for seven years, and he'd seen 150 of his colleagues murdered by the *narcotraficantes* nationwide. Five hundred judges had resigned last year alone in lieu of martyrdom for what appeared to be a failing cause.

So much for justice in Colombia.

Gallon himself had pondered resignation more than once. It would be simple to avoid the risk by stepping down, allowing someone else to hear the drug-related cases and pass sentence . . . if he dared. A wise man would refuse to sacrifice himself for a society gone mad, where criminals dictated policy and the authorities were forced to hide themselves away like rabbits waiting for a hungry predator to pass them by.

It was a national disgrace, but where did one begin to work a change? For Julio Gallon the courtroom was his chosen battlefield, and he wouldn't surrender while the slightest shred of hope remained. Not while another decent man remained to help him stand against the dealers, with their money and their guns.

The threats had been their first mistake.

Gallon had nearly given up his post the year before when Helmut Esmeral—a fellow jurist and his closest friend in Bogotá—was vaporized by an explosive charge planted under the hood of his car. The fear had set Gallon to thinking then. And drinking. He'd penned a rough draft of his resignation and was polishing the final paragraph next morning when the note arrived. *You could be next. Resign or die.*

In retrospect he wondered whether it was courage, simple stubbornness or blind machismo that compelled him to remain. If he hadn't been challenged to his face, his manhood questioned by the scum who made their homes in Medellín, Gallon would almost certainly have packed it in by now, returning to the private practice he'd enjoyed before appointment to the bench in 1983. There would have been no shame in leaving, if the resignation was his own idea, but he couldn't abide the thought of being driven out by men who made their living from the misery of others.

Gallon had worried most about his wife, but she'd borne up well beneath the strain. Her courage humbled him, but he could see the haunted look sometimes, a shadow in her eyes that gave away the lurking fear. And for the first time in their thirteen years of marriage he was thankful they were childless. It reduced the pressure points his enemies could use to break him down.

All finished for the day, Gallon took time to lock his desk and filing cabinets—not that it would stop a dedicated thief or spy—and took the time to check himself against the mirror on the inside of his closet door. He was still fit at thirty-nine, with just a trace of gray around the temples, an intriguing complement to cool gray eyes.

His bodyguards were waiting in the hallway, and they watched him double-lock his private office, one in front of him and one behind as they proceeded to the elevator. One of them was new, he thought, but it was difficult to keep the names and faces straight. Police were killed or driven from their jobs more frequently than judges in Colombia, and he wasn't inclined to ask about new faces on the team.

Downstairs the guards preceded him outside, the new man stepping to his left and checking out the sidewalk, his companion moving toward the car. When it was running Julio Gallon pushed through the swing doors and crossed the twenty feet of open pavement to the waiting vehicle.

His hand was on the door latch when it struck him that the new man should have been behind him, sticking close. He turned, a frown already forming on his face, and froze as he beheld the new guard standing in the middle of the sidewalk, feet apart, a compact submachine gun leveled at his waist.

It seemed to take forever—the explosions, bullets smacking into flesh and metal, pain that was beyond pain, shorting out his senses as he fell.

The shooting continued as he lay in the gutter, staring at the concrete smeared with blood. The shouts and sirens, when they came, were miles away and fading fast.

Gallon's last thoughts were of his wife at home, and there was barely time for him to speak her name before he closed his eyes.

Atlanta, Georgia

RALPH HATCHER KNEW things lately. He'd known the bailiffs would be watching out for guns that afternoon in the Atlanta courtroom, so he detoured to the washroom, where he used a penknife on the paper towel dispenser, squeezed the snub-nosed .38 inside and locked it again. He wouldn't be that long in court, and there was no way for the gun to drop out through that little slot, even if some guy used a hundred towels to dry his hands.

Ralph knew about the weapons check, just like he knew Márquez would walk that afternoon. He wasn't psychic, but there were times when any schmuck with one good eye and half a brain could see the bad news coming from a mile away.

For Hatcher it had started back around the time his baby died. Ramona hadn't *really* been a baby. Fifteen was damn near an adult these days, with everything a kid picked up at school and on the street.

Looking back, the street was where it all began to come apart on Hatcher. He drove a cab long hours to support his wife and child, except that Sheila had a roving eye, the bitch, and she had left him flat one weekend with an eight-year-old to raise.

The street was waiting when his little girl got old enough to look at boys and run around all night, while Ralph was out there breaking his back to pay the mortgage, keep some decent food in the refrigerator.

He did his best, but in the end the street had introduced his baby to cocaine.

The county called her death an accidental overdose, but Ralph knew murder when it looked him in the eye. He *saw* things now with a sudden clarity that made him realize he'd been blind all his life. The one thing he couldn't see was who had sold his little girl the poison that had taken her life, but that was immaterial. In time the street had given him an answer to his prayers.

You only had to listen and you knew Felipe Márquez was big in coke, some kind of ace accountant for the super dealers extradited from Colombia for trial in the United States. It might have been a fluke that he was in Atlanta, or it might have been fate's guiding hand. Whichever, Ralph had seen and suffered too damn much to let a golden opportunity slip by.

It would have been a different story if the Feds were on the ball, but they had fumbled with a major witness, left him out there in the cold where anything could happen. And, of course, it did. Now they were looking at dismissal of the charges or a lesser count that would allow Márquez to post some kind of bond before he walked.

And once the bastard walked, Ralph knew damn well that Márquez would fly. They wouldn't bag his ass so easily a second time, no sir.

Unless somebody nailed him first.

The frisk was thorough, going in, but Hatcher didn't mind because it was a lady cop and she was kind of cute. He sat through the preliminaries and the warm-up, turning off his mind to all the legalese you needed extra years of school to understand. It didn't mean a damn thing, anyway, with Márquez sitting there and grinning at his lawyer, knowing he was almost home free.

Ralph listened as the gray-haired judge dismissed the charges, taking time to rag the Feds awhile about their negligence. He didn't wait around to hear it all, but slipped outside while everyone was staring at the prosecutor, watching him go pale, then red, and finally purple in his helpless rage. The deputies let Hatcher pass, assuming he was someone from the papers, taking off to scoop the competition with a story on the case.

Two minutes in the washroom, max, and Hatcher had the .38 tucked in his belt as he emerged. Márquez and his attorneys breezed down the corridor like heroes, flashbulbs popping, minicams recording every smile and wink for history.

Ralph didn't bother smiling as he shouldered through the crowd, the pistol now in his hand. A couple of the newshawks cursed him for being pushy, but they didn't see the gun. Not yet.

Márquez was different. Living with it all these years, the fear of it, he knew exactly what was coming, and he lost his cocky smile as Hatcher pressed the .38 against his gut.

"You lousy fuck."

They knocked him to the ground before he squeezed off number four, and Hatcher let the pistol go. His job was done, and he could smile now as they got the handcuffs on his wrists and hauled him to his feet. The minicams were everywhere, and he could see right through them to thousands of different living rooms.

"There's justice for you," Hatcher told the cameras. "Fucking-A."

Ríohacha, Colombia

BEFORE HE STEPPED into the pit the young man paused to tuck a bitter coca leaf inside his mouth, adjusting it for comfort between his cheek and gum. The small gourd on his belt was filled with lime, produced by burning seashells gathered on the beach near Santa Marta, and a slender stick protruded from the top. The young man used his tongue to wet the stick. He returned it to the gourd and brought it out again with powder caked around the tip. It helped to cut the bitter coca taste and would increase the stimulating power of the drug as he went back to work.

The pit was nine feet wide and twenty feet in length, lined with strong black plastic and filled with coca leaves bobbing in a solution of water and sulfuric acid. Four times a day the young man stepped in barefoot, with the mildly caustic fluid lapping at his thighs, and briskly stirred the leaves around in their solution.

It was skilled labor, of a sort, and Gabriel Acero was content. His weekly income doubled what he used to make at home when he was working coffee on the slopes outside of Envidado. All for wading in the muck four times a day and rinsing it off before the acid had a chance to do its worst.

In three days the grayish fluid from the pit would be drawn off in plastic buckets, mixed and stirred with gasoline, more acid, other chemicals to finally produce *la merca*—the merchandise. In granulated form the cocaine base was seventy-five percent pure, the ten-acre farm yielding an average of thirty pounds per year. A thousand pounds of coca leaves yielded one pound of base.

The ivory-colored powder was worth its weight in gold. Or blood.

Acero saved his money, sending home a little every month to help his parents pay their bills and dreaming of the day when he could buy a small farm of his own—a few more years, if he was frugal and his brothers chose to share expenses on the deal.

He knew there was trouble in the cities, more with the United States, where gringos dealt cocaine with one hand and pretended to reject it with the other, but Acero had no time to waste examining the state of world affairs. He was protected on the job by his employer's payoffs to police and revolutionaries who patrolled the Magdalena district on their own. He'd be safe unless another war broke out among the *mágicos*—the major dealers—and Acero knew that only God could help him then.

For now it was enough to stand beside the pit and smell the heady reek of fermentation, knowing that his future and the future of his children yet unborn resided in cocaine. The drug was nature's miracle, and any man would be a fool to piss on a golden opportunity.

Whatever else he might have been young Gabriel Acero was no fool.

Detroit, Michigan

"FIVE DOLLARS, home boy, you be flyin'."

Pocketing the money, Cletus Todd produced a plastic vial containing two small chips of crack. The vial changed hands.

"That's it?"

"Nice doin' business with ya, man. Go on, get your rocks off now."

The skinny nine-year-old looked vaguely disillusioned as he walked away, like he was counting on a kilo for his lousy five.

No problem. Once he got that crack inside himself he'd be coming back for more, as sure as shit, and he'd steal or sell his baby sister on the street to keep it happening. It was a simple fact of life that kept a man like Cletus Todd in classy threads, with rubber on the road.

Relaxing in the back seat of his BMW, with his muscle at the wheel, it felt so good that Cletus wondered why he hadn't climbed on board the gravy train before. He thought of all the time he'd wasted being straight and hanging out around the school, his mama's church, like there was something more the world could teach him once he had it made.

He was a hero in the neighborhood, with slick designer clothes and heavy gold around his neck, the flash of diamonds on his hands. Time was, the ladies used to look at Cletus Todd and smile indulgently—or sometimes laugh out loud—but they were begging for it now. They couldn't get enough of Cletus and his sweet rock candy, bending over backward just to keep him feeling generous.

Nice work if you could get it, and he didn't give a damn about the preachers saying he was on his way to hell. The kind of people Cletus figured had a lock on heaven, he was glad to pass and let them sing their sorry fucking hymns to someone else. It didn't take a genius to decide that they were facing life ass-backward, making it a drag when it was meant to be a squeal.

Of course, you had to watch the cops sometimes, but that was cool. It turned him on to see the bagmen with their hands out, hating him and knowing they couldn't let it show, or he might cut a deal with someone else and leave them sucking wind.

"Pull over there."

The muscle followed directions like a robot and parked the car flush against the curb outside a playground. A couple of kids recognized his wheels and nudged a couple of others, a wad of cash appearing in no time.

A fifty-dollar sale this time, and things were looking up. Let all those fucking home boys taste his wares, and every one of them would be his steady customer this time next week. When they were in too deep to turn around, a small adjustment in the price would put things right.

He checked the Rolex on his wrist and found that it was creeping up on noon. He felt like eating out and picked a restaurant at random, issuing directions to the hulk behind the wheel. They didn't have a reservation, but the maître d' would find a table quick enough when Cletus flashed his winning smile and laid a twenty on the man.

He felt like celebrating, but he knew he should save the rest of it for midnight when his birthday officially began.

Twelve hours were left before the candy man turned seventeen years old.

A night drop over a jungle could be terrifying, but the Executioner had done it a hundred times before. He knew precisely when to pull the rip cord and allow his chute to open, black on black against the midnight sky. If enemy gunners were watching, they'd be distracted by the sound of Jack Grimaldi's plane—another shadow, running dark. By the time they gave it up, Mack Bolan should be on the ground.

Or close, at any rate.

His basic problem was the trees. Without a clear LZ to shoot for he was forced to take his chances, navigating by the Río Magdalena and correcting so that he didn't wind up in the water, weighed down by his gear and smothered by his parachute. The target wasn't perfect, by a long shot, and he knew a thousand different things could still go wrong— from twisted ankles to a sniper waiting on the riverbank— but it wasn't as if the soldier had a choice.

The probe was mandatory, and it couldn't be delayed.

Correcting, Bolan used the left-hand risers to control his drift, as the river and surrounding forest rushed up to meet him. He could see already that their calculations had been overgenerous. The wide parts of the riverbank were barely fifteen feet across, and much of it was overhung by trees cut off from Bolan's bird's-eye view.

At sixty feet he made a new correction, but the wind came out of nowhere, driving Bolan to the left before he had a chance to compensate. It saved him from the river, but it also drove his chute into the trees and pinned him there.

The first jolt nearly took his breath away, but he recovered swiftly, calculating distance and the angle of the drop. The rocky soil was close to twenty feet below him, and he didn't like the odds of plummeting directly to earth without some damage to his legs or spine. Instead, he took a moment to examine his surroundings—canopy and shroud lines were tangled in the branches of a venerable tree—and knew that he'd have to climb.

The warrior scrambled up the giant spiderweb without unfastening his harness, banking on it for insurance if he slipped and fell. When he reached a sturdy limb, he straddled it and flicked the quick-release clasps, shrugging off the straps that had secured his parachute. On any normal drop he'd have taken time to hide the chute, or even bury it, but there was nothing he could do about the tangled, tattered canopy from where he sat.

It took him several moments to descend, avoiding noise that might have given him away to anyone within a radius of fifty yards. The moment that his feet touched Mother Earth, he flicked the safety off his CAR-15 and held the weapon ready, covering the shadows that surrounded him.

No hostile movement.

No response of any kind.

He had the best part of a mile to travel in the darkness, and he checked his compass first to verify directions. Medellín was west, the Río Magdalena flowed north and Bolan's destination fell between the two. He'd been briefed with maps and aerial photography, but it was worthless when you were on the ground surrounded by forest and your enemies.

A mile was nothing over open ground, but it became a challenge in the jungle when you found yourself in hostile territory. From the moment his feet had left the aircraft, hurtling through space, the warrior had known there was no one he could trust, regardless of sex or age, the uniform worn. Smart money said his enemy had managed to corrupt or terrorize the local population thoroughly, assassinating those he couldn't hire or bribe. Police and peasants, military personnel and revolutionaries sworn to overthrow the ruling government—all listened when money talked.

That made it solo all the way, and Bolan knew the moves by heart. Avoiding native settlements as if they were infected with the plague, he had to make his way northwest past any sentries or patrols along the way and penetrate the compound where his target manufactured poison by the ton. He wouldn't find the man himself—the viper's lair was north of Medellín, along the Río Nechi—but he didn't plan to tag the enemy tonight.

It was supposed to be a soft probe, in and out, with information as the goal. No fuss, no muss, if everything proceeded in accordance with his master plan.

The village was a landmark, and he found it half an hour after touching down. All was quiet at a glance, but then he made the sentries, one each on the north and south. They were young men with ancient rifles—Springfields, by their look—but they could still do lethal damage in a marksman's hands. Aside from the potential risk of injury or death, Bolan didn't care to give himself away by trading shots with Indians before he reached his destination. He took pains to circle wide around the settlement, avoiding contact with the guards.

He'd been warned about the opposition's first line of defense, the local residents who made a living stripping coca leaves and therefore had a stake in guaranteeing that the operation went on, unmolested. If the information in his briefing was correct, the Indians received a bonus—paid in cash or cocaine base, their choice—each time they bagged an interloper in the area and brought his head to their employers. Failing that, if they were taken by surprise or physically outnumbered, every village in the area had been equipped with walkie-talkies to alert the standby troops.

From this point on he'd be forced to watch out for guerrillas on patrol. Colombia was home to more than 140 paramilitary groups, both right and left, and most were flexible enough to sacrifice their "sacred principles" by taking payoffs from the drug cartels. At any given time the major cocaine labs might be protected by a flying squad of Communists or neofascists, all of them well armed and anxious for an opportunity to use their hardware on a living target.

Bolan was rigged for war—complete with automatic rifle, side arms, extra ammunition and grenades—but he was hoping for a chance to scrutinize the opposition quietly without a major confrontation to reveal his presence in the area.

The warrior met the first patrol a quarter mile southeast of his intended destination. He flattened himself behind a fallen log and counted off an even dozen soldiers as they passed. They weren't taking any pains to keep the noise down. Bolan let them go and hoped the rest of them were as negligent in the performance of their duties. It would make life easier if he could count on careless enemies ahead.

When they were gone, the voices fading out of earshot, Bolan got his act into gear. Perimeter surveillance meant that he was getting close, and in another twenty minutes he could pick out lights ahead in the near distance.

From three hundred yards out he began to watch for booby traps along the game trail he was following. When he'd closed the gap to fifty yards, Bolan realized the compound occupants had let themselves relax. Their guards were posted and they knew the fix was in; what more could any self-respecting dealer ask?

He circled the perimeter, deciding on an angle of approach that took the roving guards into account. There were five men he could see, with something like a hundred yards of ground for each to cover as they ambled back and forth, their automatic weapons slung or carried in the crooks of slender arms. They seemed alert enough, but there was simply too much forest, too many shadows for a five-man team to do the job.

The warrior chose his moment, waiting for a pair of sentries to connect and kill some time in conversation as they walked their separate beats. The shadows covered Bolan as he broke from cover, dodging over open ground with one eye on the guards and sliding into welcome shadows at the north end of a prefab barracks block. He noted lights, heard voices speaking Spanish through an open window and decided there were at least half a dozen men inside.

Across the compound pits with plastic liners reeked like a moonshine camp. Two jeeps were parked beside an army surplus half-ton truck. The vehicles would be of use transporting men and merchandise along the narrow, rutted track that Bolan's map showed running south in the direction of Sonson, some fifty miles away. He saw another barracks block beyond the one that sheltered him, some equipment sheds and a slit latrine. That was it.

Construction of a camp like this would cost his opposition next to nothing in materials and labor, but the Executioner was looking at a gold mine. Twice a week the pits gave up their bounty to be treated and processed into cocaine base, then it was driven south to the refineries where base became cocaine and was prepared for shipment north to the United States and Western Europe. If the camp was blown somehow, a new one would be thrown up somewhere else within a week.

The game went on as long as there were millions to be made.

Or make that *billions* now. Drug money accounted for an estimated ten percent of Colombia's gross national product, roughly equal to the country's yearly expenditure on imports, while the average Colombian citizen limped along with a gross income of $1,100 per year. That kind of drug money purchased guns and loyalty, politicians and police. Assassins could be hired for ten or fifteen dollars on the streets of Medellín, where human life came cheaper than a round of drinks.

The warrior would have liked a glimpse inside the honcho's office, but he knew that would be pushing it. He hadn't come to gather evidence for an indictment, but to gauge security and test the waters for a later assault. So far the toughest part appeared to be a hazardous approach past jungle villages and checkpoints, with the roving bands of left- and right-wing gunmen serving as uncounted jokers in the deck.

A scuffling of feet behind him put the soldier on alert, just in time to slip a hand beneath his arm and palm the sleek Beretta 93-R with its custom silencer attached. He never knew exactly where the gunner came from, but the guy was there, no more than twenty feet away and closing on a hard collision course. He hadn't sighted Bolan yet, but there was no place for the Executioner to hide.

A choice, then.

He could drop the guy at once on open ground, or let him move a little closer, risking confrontation and alarm before he made the tag. The gunner had an AK-47, right hand wrapped around the pistol grip, the muzzle down, but Bolan couldn't tell about the safety or a ready finger on the trigger.

Take the chance.

He waited, counting down the doomsday numbers, the Beretta sighted on his target as the sentry closed it up, eyes downcast.

Another yard . . .

The guy looked up, saw Bolan and died without a chance to figure out exactly why. The single parabellum round drilled through his forehead, and he collapsed.

It had to be a simple reflex, Bolan thought, that made his finger clench around the AK-47's trigger, ripping off a half magazine before he hit the ground. The slugs went nowhere, chewing up the earth and hacking through the dead man's foot, but the racket was enough to bring the whole camp down on Bolan's head.

No time for subtlety from this point on. He holstered the Beretta, took a firm grip on his CAR-15 and sprinted for the jeeps. It was a long shot, granted, but he stood no chance at all on foot, with better than a dozen guns behind him and walkie-talkies broadcasting the alert to hunting parties in the forest all around. His one chance—if it was a chance—would be to hit the road with wheels and try to ditch the tail before he reached Sonson.

Behind him someone fired a submachine gun burst, and Bolan took the time to answer with his automatic carbine, catching one surprised defender and blowing him away. More guns joined in, but he couldn't stop to duel them. The odds were too long already, and the more time Bolan spent beneath the lights, the better chance some sniper had of getting lucky.

Keys hung in the ignition, and Bolan reckoned there was little risk of auto theft out here in *narcotraficante* land. He hunched behind the wheel to minimize their target as he turned the engine over, urging it to catch, rewarded with a healthy snarl from underneath the hood. In front of him the windshield frosted over, quivered for a microsecond, then imploded, spraying him with bits of glass.

The Executioner returned fire with his CAR-15, not bothering to aim. It was enough to keep them down until he had a fair head start. There was no way to stop the enemy from following, but Bolan still had one or two tricks up his sleeve, if he could only catch them on the trail.

The compound had no gate, per se, but a guardhouse had been constructed on the perimeter beside the narrow road. A pair of gunners had the exit covered as he made his move, one each on right and left, both armed with M-16s and firing for effect.

If they were half the marksmen they pretended to be, Bolan would have been in trouble. But both were anxious, frightened or excited by the smell of blood, and their initial bursts were high and low respectively. It was the only chance that they would ever have, and they had blown it.

Bolan shot the gunner on his left, a burst that punched him over backward in a boneless sprawl. Before he lifted off the trigger, the warrior swung the jeep to intercept his second adversary, knowing he could never swing the CAR-15 around in time to make it work.

The gunner saw it coming and bolted, but it was a hopeless contest from the start. Bolan caught him with the starboard fender, riding out the double jolt as two wheels mowed him down.

The Colombians chased the Executioner with a storm of automatic gunfire, but it was mostly wasted in the dark. He heard a round or two strike home—the tailgate and the extra fuel can—but he kept his lights off for a quarter mile and left them guessing where to aim. A sharp bend in the road allowed some breathing room, and Bolan flicked his lights on then, accelerating through a midnight tunnel formed by overhanging trees.

Three minutes later, give or take, there were headlights in his rearview mirror, making up lost time. They'd be with him all the way, he knew, unless they shot him off the road...or he could find a way to stop them first.

Bolan rounded another curve and saw his opportunity ahead. He poured it on, his lead extended to a full half mile before he found a turnout, shifted down and cut off the lights. He left the engine running, with the parking brake engaged, as he went EVA, a frag grenade in one hand and his CAR-15 in the other.

Timing was the key. He heard the enemy approaching, trusting in experience to compensate for their excessive speed, and he released the safety pin on his grenade before he saw their headlights flash around the curve. The jeep was in front, with four passengers, the half-ton close behind.

A simple underhand was all it took, and five seconds lead time. The jeep was closing in on his turnout when a ball of fire erupted underneath and rolled it into the middle of the track. He had a glimpse of airborne bodies as he raised the CAR-15 and sighted on the half-ton's windshield, squeezing off a short precision burst.

With a dead man at the steering wheel, there was no way for them to miss the pileup. Initial impact pushed the jeep along for ten or fifteen yards before the truck veered off and wrapped its grille around a tree. The gunners piling out from underneath the tarp were shaken, wobbling around on rubber legs, and Bolan stitched them with a magazine of 5.56 mm tumblers, lobbing in another frag grenade to make it stick.

He didn't know if all of them were dead; it didn't matter, either way. Pursuit was stalled, and even if there was another vehicle around the camp, a new team would be forced to clear the road before it could proceed. By that time Bolan would be miles away and closing in on his rendezvous. A signal to Grimaldi for the pickup would take them both away from Medellín and their enemies.

2

It never failed. The aerial approach to Stony Man Farm was breathtaking, a low-level sweep along the Blue Ridge chain with the Shenandoah Valley and the Alleghenies to the west. Clear skies soared above and evergreens below as Jack Grimaldi brought them in.

"It's a little different here."

Mack Bolan understood the reference to their swift evacuation from Colombia and nodded.

"All the difference in the world."

The airstrip didn't look like much, but it was up to spec for military fighter planes and small civilian aircraft. The crew assigned to maintenance took pride in making it look dusty and unused, occasionally leaving farm machinery parked across the east-west runway when guests weren't expected. It helped with the illusion and prevented uninvited visitors from dropping in out of the blue.

There would be no obstructions this time with Grimaldi cleared to land at noon.

"Two minutes."

Bolan spotted the Farm, rolling green surrounded by the forest on three sides, its buildings set well back and out of sight from Skyline Drive. The place was posted, and any prowler who got past the chain-link fence and razor wire would have to face a stiff interrogation . . . if he lived.

The landing was a no-frills textbook exercise, and Bolan saw a Blazer start out from the house and make tracks in their direction. He didn't recognize the driver, but it came as no surprise. Rotation of the ground staff was routine, and it had been a while since Bolan had paid a visit to the Farm.

"Good afternoon, sir."

A salute for Bolan, which was shared with Jack Grimaldi since the driver had no fix upon his rank. A pair of "farmhands" were approaching on a tractor, sent to fuel the plane and tuck it safely out of sight before they went about their standard rounds. The Blazer jockey opened Bolan's door and waited for him to have a seat before he slid behind the wheel.

The Farm affected Bolan different ways at different times. There were so many ghosts and echoes from the days when he was working with the government full-time, before a traitor had ripped his world apart. Old business, long behind him now, but never quite forgotten. Sometimes Bolan couldn't wait to catch a glimpse of Stony Man; at other times, once there, he couldn't wait to get away.

Brognola met them on the porch, with Leo Turrin at his side. The helicopter ride from Washington had left them slightly rumpled, but Bolan thought they both looked well.

"Nice trip?" the head Fed asked.

"As always. Is everybody here?"

"Downstairs. You need to freshen up or anything?"

"I'll pass."

Bolan and Grimaldi entered through a coded access door, left open when Brognola went out to meet them on the porch. Another granted access to the Farm's computer room, a necessary hike to reach the elevator that would take them down one flight to basement level and the other people they'd come to see. Two minutes later they were in the war room, looking at a king-size conference table lined with padded chairs, most of which were occupied.

The Executioner smiled at Aaron Kurtzman, aka "Bear." As Stony Man's librarian and master of the data systems, Kurtzman would be more or less responsible for any information they received that afternoon. The wheelchair hadn't slowed him down a bit, and in effect he ran the Farm with help from Barbara Price, the honey-blonde who sat immediately to his left.

Bolan had a warm smile for Barbara, remembering the stolen moments they'd shared on his last few visits to the Farm. He saw the color rising in her cheeks and felt himself responding, holding it in check until the proper time.

The four new arrivals took their places at the table. On Bolan's right Bear and Barbara shared their side with Able Team, three fighting men the Executioner had known forever, from the kickoff of his lonely war against the odds. Two of them, Hermann Schwarz and Rosario Blancanales, went back to the Pen Team Able days in Vietnam where Bolan had earned his nickname with a sniper's rifle and a willingness to hunt his enemies the way some other men stalked deer and elk. They called Schwarz "Gadgets" back in those days, and it had stuck, a tribute to his skill with booby traps, bugs, transistors—nearly anything at all. Rosario, for his part, had become "Politician," after his ability to soothe the ruffled feathers of the brass or calm a frightened native with a few well-chosen words. Together, after Bolan's blast at Malibu, they'd become the hottest P.I.s in the business, but they'd dropped it in a flash when Bolan and Brognola summoned them to the Phoenix Program at Stony Man.

Carl Lyons had been working LAPD's orgcrime beat when Bolan crossed his path, fresh out of Pittsfield and the first phase of his war against the Mafia, and neither man was ever quite the same again. For Lyons it had meant a transfer to the Feds and undercover work as he'd joined forces with the two survivors of the early Bolan "Death Squad" to pursue the savages wherever they were found. His nickname—"Iron Man"—described the warrior side of Lyons, but it failed to note the depth of his compassion where the hapless victims were involved.

To Bolan's left the men of Phoenix Force had taken seats without regard to rank. The nearest, Calvin James, was still the new man on the team, a black Chicago native with a knack for languages and underwater demolition work—the latter specialty acquired while serving with the U.S. Navy SEALs. He smiled and tipped a nonexistent hat to Bolan as the Executioner sat down.

Immediately next to James was the senior member of the team, Yakov Katzenelenbogen, the Israeli veteran of Mossad. It took a second glance to spot the excellent prosthetic arm—his right—and even then a novice wouldn't detect the .22-caliber surprise built into the index finger of his artificial hand. Mid-fifties, tan and fit, he favored Bolan with a smile and lit a fresh unfiltered Camel cigarette, waiting for the briefing to begin.

The Cuban, Rafael Encizo, had the features of an Indian and a childhood scar below his mouth. Other scars, inflicted by interrogators at Principe Prison, didn't show when he was dressed unless you looked behind the dark brown eyes. He cast a sour glance at Katzenelenbogen, wrinkling his nose against the cloud of cigarette smoke, then relaxed and let it go, acknowledging the new arrivals with a nod.

Beside Encizo Gary Manning sipped a mug of steaming coffee, raising it to Bolan almost as a toast. The tall Canadian had ruddy cheeks and gray eyes that were alternately warm or cold as flint, depending on his mood. An engineer who specialized in stress mechanics, he'd learned the demolition business from his father, polishing his skills in military service where he qualified as expert with explosives and small arms.

Last up was David McCarter, a Sandhurst graduate who had resigned his commission in the Glosters Division of the British army to serve with the SAS on antiterrorist duty. An expert pilot and rally driver, McCarter's casual bearing and ready smile masked a deep-seated suspicion of his fellow-man, expressed on occasion in flashes of temper. This afternoon the smile was on, McCarter recognizing that his closest friends on earth were gathered in the conference room.

Brognola broke the ice. "We all know why we're here, I take it?"

"Someone hit the panic button," Lyons quipped.

"You're close. The White House war on drugs has hit a snag, to put it mildly. They've been cranking bureaucratic studies out like there's no tomorrow, handing down indictments for the big boys out of country, but the net result on imports has been zip. You'll hear about new seizures every time you watch TV, but I'm reliably informed that customs and the DEA are bagging less than ten percent of what's been coming in."

"Does that include the twenty tons they busted in Chicago?" Blancanales asked.

"That pickup was a fluke," Brognola replied, "but off the record, yes. The quote on ten percent or less includes Chicago."

"Geez."

Gary Manning raised a hand. "What progress on the extraditions?"

"Slim to none. Officially Colombian authorities are doing everything they can to bag a dozen of the honchos we've got paper on, but they've been getting nowhere fast. Some of the problem has to be corruption, but the violence they've experienced down there would also seem to indicate a serious attempt to clean the bastards out. They just don't have the muscle for the job."

"And we're supposed to save the play?" Grimaldi sounded skeptical at best.

"We're looking for a handle," Brognola told him. "If we can spike the operation hard enough to shake them up, we might just turn the game around and let the home team win one for a change. It's worth a shot, and Striker's done some ground work for us on the scene."

All eyes turned to Bolan. Then Calvin James asked, "How'd it go?"

"It went. I didn't get the soft probe I was hoping for, but with a little luck I'm hoping Mr. Big'll blame it on the competition."

"Decent chance," Brognola said. "The cartels have been working overtime on a united front, but it's a joke. With 250 million dollars on the table every month, you can imagine that the competition's fierce. In Medellín alone they average better than a hundred homicides per day, and roughly half of those are drug related. If anybody tells you the cartels have pulled together under stress, they're feeding you a line."

"Sounds like they're bent on killing one another off without our help," Schwarz observed.

"I wish. The fact is, the shooters haven't tagged a major boss in the past ten years. They're hitting runners, whole-sale buyers, button men, informants—and they've got a couple of dozen wanna-be's on tap for every slug that buys it. Like the song says, easy money's got a very strong lure."

"That's *easy?*" Katzenelenbogen didn't sound amused.

"Compared to picking coffee beans and pulling down twelve hundred bucks a year, you bet it is. All set to meet the opposition, Bear?"

"Affirmative."

The lights went down as Kurtzman keyed his console, and a screen descended from the ceiling at Brognola's back. A slide projector mounted in the facing wall clicked on, and they were treated to a smiling candid shot of a Hispanic man in his early forties, stylish hair and clothes, his eyes concealed behind a pair of mirrored shades.

"Luis Costanza," Brognola said. "He's Mr. Big in Medellín, and no mistake. Personal fortune estimated at two billion dollars U.S. He's looking at indictments in L.A., Atlanta and New York, if anyone can ever track him down."

"He's underground?" Schwarz asked.

"Not so you'd notice. He's got digs in Bogotá and Medellín, of course—your average mansion types—but home's a seven-thousand-acre spread along the Río Nechi, with a house that makes Hearst Castle look like Dogpatch, U.S.A. We're talking crystal stairs, Italian marble, fixtures made of solid gold, a private zoo complete with elephants. Your basic narcobaron bachelor pad."

"A place like that should be open season from the likes of M19," McCarter observed.

"You'd think so," the big Fed replied, "but it appears Costanza has the local liberation armies on his payroll. Any way you figure it, they're leaving him alone. And if our information is correct, he uses them on hits from time to time."

"Like the supreme court gig?" Grimaldi asked.

"A case in point. Ninety-five dead in one sitting, including eleven supreme court justices, and left-wing revolutionaries got the credit. We're convinced that dealers out of Medellín picked up the tab, and we have confirmation that several extradition files were burned before the military flushed out the hit team. Publicity and cash for the guerrillas, cover and convenience for the men on top of the cartel."

The picture changed to a slender, scowling face with numbers underneath.

"Esteban Ortega," Brognola announced. "Costanza's number two in Medellín, arrested nineteen times with one conviction on a charge of petty theft. He handles wet work, and the word is that he likes to take a hand himself. Enjoys it, so I'm told."

"He has the look," McCarter said.

"With this one looks can kill. We've made him as the trigger on a minimum of thirty-seven homicides, and roughly half of those are since he hit the big time. He doesn't like to let his troops have all the fun."

"Nice guy."

"Indictments in Miami and New York for drug-related homicides. Two cops included in the charges out of Florida. They're set to fry him, if they ever get the chance."

"And if they don't?" Grimaldi asked.

"Dead's dead. Let's see what we can do." Brognola shot a glance at Kurtzman. "How about the not-so-friendly opposition?"

"Coming up."

The next face on the screen was round, with heavy jowls and mirror-imaged chins above an open collar.

"This one is José Mercado. Number two in terms of yearly income from cocaine, and you can bet he's trying harder to be number one. Mercado also operates from Medellín, with offices in Bogotá. He joined Costanza a few months back in declaring war against the government, but life goes on and they've been sniping at each other ever since."

"The more things change," Katz said, "the more they stay the same."

"Next up, Raul Rodriguez. He's based in Bogotá, and we rate him number three behind Mercado, and the two of them are fairly tight . . . at least as far as knocking off Costanza is concerned. If they succeed, the chances are they'll start in on each other, but I'd rather that they didn't get the chance."

"You're looking at our wedge," Bolan said. "Play Mercado and Rodriguez off against Costanza, and there's a decent chance we can tie them up and keep them occupied until we make the tag."

"Who's tagging whom?" McCarter asked.

"A sweep across the board would be ideal," Brognola answered, "but we'll take what we can get. Costanza has priority. The rest is gravy."

"Sounds more like blood pudding."

"Either way. I have to tell you we've got jokers in the deck."

On cue a broad, familiar face filled the screen—sharp eyes beneath a braided military cap, with heavy brows, a gap-toothed smile and pockmarks on the cheeks.

"Well, shit."

Brognola glanced at Calvin James and smiled. "You called it right. General Hector Mendoza Caseros, esteemed president of Panama. If you've been conscious in the past two years, you've heard about his links to the cartel. At one time or another he's permitted every major dealer in Colombia to take 'vacations' in his country under military guard against 'harassment' by American or their own authorities. Aside from that, Costanza and his competition have been shipping product out of Panama to beat the customs crunch in Bogotá. Caseros didn't fill those Swiss accounts of his by saving pesos from his presidential salary, and he's not about to sever his cartel connections while the goose keeps laying golden eggs."

"The last I heard," Katz said, "it was official hands-off on Caseros."

"So it is *officially*. But everybody and his brother knows the White House wants Caseros out. We haven't been cleared for executive action, per se, but if the general should have an accident related to his drug connections, don't expect a lot of tears in Washington. The main thing is, we need a solid handle on his links with the cartel, in case of any comebacks on the deal."

"How solid?" Manning asked.

Brognola shrugged. "It wouldn't have to stand in court, but we'll need something for the press to chew on, and enough to satisfy congressional committees with a dim view of covert involvement on the foreign front."

"You mentioned jokers, plural," Blancanales said.

"That's right. The next two faces are Israeli, ex-Mossad, now working in the private sector."

Split-screen images showed a fairly young man on the right with modish hair and winning smile, and his partner, on the left, in his fifties, with a salt-and-pepper military buzz, an eye patch and a scar that snaked across his cheek to meet the corner of his thin-lipped mouth.

"I know the eye patch," Katzenelenbogen said, his voice an angry rumble. "Isaac Auerbach. We were together in the Six Day War. He lost the eye one afternoon before I lost my arm. A piece of shrapnel."

"That's our boy," Brognola replied, confirming the ID. "Our reading is that he was separated from Mossad on grounds of 'policy.' In other words, his views on execution and interrogation of the enemy surpassed what Tel Aviv was willing to abide. For the past six years or so he's been involved in training mercenaries, private armies—anything that doesn't jeopardize Israeli interests or directly aid the Palestinian resistance. On the right, Chaim Feldman, junior partner in the firm they call Trans-Global Security Consultants."

"How does Auerbach tie in with the cartel?" Katz demanded.

"Sometime ago a group of wealthy farmers in the Río Magdalena valley filed complaints that they were catching hell from Communist guerrillas in the countryside—kidnappings, homicides, you name it."

"Farmers?" Calvin James was frowning as he spoke. "Are we supposed to guess what they were growing?"

"Some of them were cattlemen and coffee growers," Brognola replied, "but you're on target, anyway. Costanza and Mercado chipped in big to hire security consultants, and they picked Trans-Global. By the time our buddies finished polishing the troops, their rebel opposition didn't have a prayer. Coincidentally it was around that time that some of the rebels saw the light and started working part-time for Costanza—in the name of liberation, if you're buying that."

"Trans-Global's still around?"

"Damn straight. These days they operate a training school outside Medellín, ostensibly to help executive chauffeurs protect their clientele. In fact, they train *sicarios*—a special breed of two-wheel shooters—in the fine points of assassination using motorbikes and automatic weapons. It's become an artform, in Colombia. If you hear a Honda coming, hit the deck. The honchos spend a lot of time in Panama, where they can watch their numbered bank accounts."

"I want him," Katzenelenbogen said, eyes locked on the smiling likeness of his former comrade.

"Sold. We're splitting up our force to maximize the coverage, Phoenix working Panama for openers, while Striker and Grimaldi lay the groundwork in Colombia."

"I think you're leaving someone out," Lyons said.

"Not quite. We've got a situation in Miami ripe for Able. Seems Costanza's got a local representative who's not averse to killing federal agents, witnesses, Miami cops—you name it. Street talk calls her La Araña. That's the Spider, just in case your Spanish is as bad as mine. No firm ID beyond the street name yet."

"Did you say 'her'?" McCarter asked.

Across the table Barbara Price put on an impish smile. "He did. Is there a problem, David? Something chauvinistic you might like to share?"

"No comment."

"As I thought."

"So we're on tap to squash the Spider," Lyons quipped. "I'd better take a can of Raid along."

"Take more than that. Her shooters are responsible for sixty-seven hits we know about between Miami and New Orleans. They're required to bring a finger back to verify the kill. Sometimes they pull a necktie job for show-and-tell."

"Okay, *two* cans of Raid."

Brognola let it go. "You'll each be working independently, coordinating through myself and Leo here. If anybody finishes ahead of schedule, we can try and fit you on Striker's end."

"And speaking of the schedule..." Leo Turrin left it open, handing off to the big Fed.

"Ten days. It isn't much, I know, but we're projecting anything beyond that time for bad news and diminishing returns."

"Ten days beginning when?" Grimaldi asked.

"Tomorrow, bright and early."

"Damn, there goes my weekend."

There were smiles around the table, most of them reserved, as Brognola prepared to shut the briefing down.

"We're not expecting miracles," he said, "but if you've got a spare one up your sleeve, it wouldn't hurt. Repeating the priorities—Costanza first, the competition if we can, Caseros if it fits." He tossed a sidelong glance at Able Team. "Whatever goes down south, we want Costanza's operation in Miami wiped, case closed."

3

"You figure they can really do it?" Leo Turrin asked.

"Depends on what you're asking," Hal Brognola answered. "If you mean turn the flow of drugs around, hell, no. But interrupt it long enough to make some bastards feel the pinch, I'd say it's possible. Take down a couple of the honchos we could never lay our hands on any other way? You bet."

"Costanza?"

"Touch and go. It's like he's got himself a whole damn country bribed and terrorized—two countries, if we throw in Panama. With those kind of odds I wouldn't want to bet the pension, either way."

"You bet ten lives," Turrin said, frowning.

"Every one of them was wide awake in there. They know their chances going in. Besides, it isn't just that they're the best we've got right now. They're *all* we've got."

"That ought to tell you something, Hal."

"It tells me what I've known for over thirty years. The politicians stay alive by rooting out problems and offering solutions to the public. Sometimes they don't have to dig so deep—the problems jump right up and smack them in the face. That makes it easy—promising, I mean. Delivering is something else."

"So this is all about another win in 1992?"

"I don't know what it means to anybody else, and I don't give a damn, okay? To me it means we're taking action that's been sadly overdue. For all I know we may be too damn late already, but we're bound to try."

"And if it goes to hell?"

"We live with it. What else?"

The answer brought a scowl to Turrin's face. Before the creation of the Phoenix team and Stony Man he'd devoted years to undercover work inside the Massachusetts Mafia, eventually rising to the rank of underboss before he'd pulled the pin. He knew what "living with it" meant; he had the act down cold. "You say that like it counts for something. Hey, we blew it, but we're big enough to live with our mistakes."

"It may be all we've got," Brognola said.

"If you feel that way, we ought to scrub the play right now."

"And then what? Maybe tell the White House, 'Sorry, if you give us something easier next time, we'll try and help you out'?"

"I don't like splitting up the team like this."

"It was the only way to go. If we try to work it piece-meal, all we do is chase the heavies back and forth from one place to another. Panama, Colombia, Miami—Timbuktu, for all I know. Ten days is stretching it, the way things are."

"Too many wild cards," Turrin said. "The business in Miami, and this thing with Auerbach and Katz."

"They'll work it out."

"So what about El General? You know the way Caseros loves to showboat for the press."

"And tell them what? That someone's checking out a link between his office and the Medellín cartel? Publicity's the last thing he'll be looking for until he's got the mess contained."

"I love it. Now we've got *two* hostile governments to deal with, plus Miami, where we don't know who we're after."

"They're not hostile in Colombia. They just can't pull their weight."

"Some of them maybe. Don't forget the cops and military officers Costanza and his cronies have been paying off for years."

"I'm not forgetting anything."

"You know how Striker feels when it comes down to firing on a uniform."

"I'm trusting him to find a way around it."

"Yeah, I know. It sucks, that's all."

"What else is new?"

"You didn't mention the Canadians, I notice."

"What's the point? Their operation hasn't been confirmed, and they'll be playing watchdog any way you cut it, if they show at all."

"Another wild card."

"Maybe. If it bothers you, I'll put a bug in Striker's ear tomorrow before he leaves."

"Couldn't hurt."

Brognola stared at Turrin for a moment, reading him the way old friends can read each other at the worst of times without communicating verbally.

"I know what's eating you," he said at last. "I feel the same damn way, but think about it, will you? Even if they don't rate fifty-fifty odds, they've got a fighting chance. Spread out, it works to our advantage in a way. We take the bastards by surprise across the board. With any luck, before Costanza knows he's being hit at home, we bag his Florida connection, maybe even foul his nest in Panama."

"With luck," Leo said bitterly. "A lousy crap shoot."

"One big difference—we're not playing."

"Sure we are. We're just not using chips."

"Okay, you want to pass? It's short, but I can still find someone else."

"Like hell. Whichever way it goes, I'm in. We live with it together."

"Well, then."

"But it doesn't mean I have to like it, Hal."

"I'd worry if you did."

"Just so you know."

"I hear you, Leo."

When he was alone, Brognola ran the slides again, examining the faces of his opposition. Seven men, each one commanding private armies to defend the territory they had eked out for themselves. Caseros had a whole damn country at his beck and call, the narcobarons running close behind with hired assassins, radical guerrillas and corrupt police prepared to pull a trigger anytime and anywhere.

The odds were shitty any way you broke them down, and that was bad enough to start with. Brognola wasn't prepared to make things worse by telling members of his team that the White House didn't know a goddamn thing about the plan—that he'd worked it up himself to counter bureaucratic stalls and paper shuffling.

And if it blew up in his face, along with men he'd come to love like sons or brothers, he'd live with it. Damn right.

The only question was, how long?

HIS ROOM WAS on the southeast corner of the second floor, complete with private bath and coded access door. The Executioner had passed on after-dinner mingling in the den downstairs, content to let himself unwind a bit and think about the days ahead.

Colombia. Costanza. One more all-or-nothing play against the cannibals.

He didn't need a crystal ball or tarot cards to know that Brognola was worried, playing all the combinations in his mind and coming up with double zero more than half the time. The big Fed was committing everything—and everyone—he had to make it work, and he'd still fall short of even money if you took the odds to any two-bit bookie on the Vegas Strip.

It wasn't suicide exactly—not like jumping off a freeway overpass with both eyes open and a semi rolling toward you at a steady sixty-five. More like the jumper had a rubber band around his ankles, counting on resiliency to save his ass before the final, crushing impact. But you couldn't trust the rubber band to bear your weight until you tried the stunt for real, and if you blew it, you were lying broken on the pavement, staring up at eighteen wheels without a hope left in the world.

No sweat.

The Executioner had made that leap before, a thousand times, and he was still around. He wondered if repetition shaved the odds in favor of his enemies or gave the warrior a survival edge, but there was no answer possible until he tried it one more time.

The soft, insistent knocking brought him back. He keyed the door and smiled at Barbara Price, blond hair cut shoulder length, her jumpsuit snug without the sprayed-on look.

"Hello again."

She entered, then waited for the door to close. "I thought we'd better talk."

"Okay."

"You've been avoiding me."

He nearly winced but caught himself and came up with "Not so."

"Let's say evading, then. You've been here five, six hours, and we haven't said a dozen words."

"It's been a while. I wasn't sure exactly what to say."

He sat on the bed and Barbara sat beside him, facing toward him, one leg cocked across her other knee. "That's it? You're tongue-tied?"

Bolan grinned despite himself. "I've had a few things on my mind."

"No good. I've been assigned as the controller on this mission. At the very least we need to be on speaking terms."

"You have to understand—"

"I do," she interrupted him. "I know that you have ghosts here. You were straight about that going in. We each have separate lives. I'm not about to ask for a commitment, Mack."

"Why shouldn't you? It's normal, Barb. Nobody ever said that working on this project meant you had to live and die alone."

She forced a smile. "That's reassuring. What about yourself?"

"Long story," Bolan answered. "Most of it you know—the names and places, anyway. The inside part of it is different. Let's just say I've seen and done too much to try to share it with a gentle soul."

"It doesn't hurt to share."

Involuntarily his mind began to run a roll call of the lost, complete with snaps before and after.

"Sometimes," Bolan told her, "sharing kills."

"I'm not that fragile, Mack."

Neither was April.

Instead of saying it he settled for a lame "I hope not."

"Are you having doubts about the mission?"

"Not per se. It's just the kind of action that can blow up in your face without a warning. When that happens—*if* it happens—I won't have the time to stop and think about the folks I left behind."

"No strings," she said. "Is that what's on your mind?"

"I'm thinking that you can't lose what you never had to start with."

"Losing's not the problem. Everybody loses something, sometime. Closing off your opportunities is something else."

He smiled. "Is that what I've been doing?"

Barbara shrugged. "I wouldn't be surprised."

She kissed him then before he had a chance to stop her or to make the move himself. Her lips were soft and warm, the first touch of her tongue reserved and tentative, encouraged by his own.

"That's better."

"Yes, it was."

"I really need a shower," Barbara told him, rising to her feet. "You want to scrub my back?"

He felt the ramparts crumbling as she drew the jumpsuit's zipper down below her waist. "I thought you'd never ask."

They ran the shower hot enough to steam. Inside, an instant flash of claustrophobia dissolved as Barbara stepped into Bolan's arms and he held her close. They got to know each other inch by inch, employing hands and mouths that never learned enough. As Bolan bathed her, soaping every inch below her chin, he felt the lady trembling with a need that matched his own.

When it was her turn, Bolan couldn't wait. He lifted her with big hands underneath her arms and pressed her back against the sweating tile. Her knees came up, legs wrapped around his waist. Barbara slipped a hand between them, guiding him. They knew it couldn't last, their rhythm almost frantic with the water beating down upon them, minds and bodies straining for release. The moment left them breathless from exertion and the steamy atmosphere inside the shower stall.

"Have mercy."

"Giving up?"

"You wish." She bit his shoulder playfully and made a small adjustment in the temperature control. "I need to breathe, is all."

"You don't like saunas?"

"For relaxing, sure. It wasn't what I had in mind."

Hair plastered to his forehead, Bolan smiled. "I wouldn't want to get your hopes up."

"So we'll work on something else."

He let her wash him, lathering his chest and shoulders, back and buttocks. For the legs she knelt before him, Bolan's body blocking out the shower spray.

"That looks uncomfortable." She soaped him with lazy strokes, half turning him to rinse.

"It can be."

"Something I can do to help?"

"I'm in your hands."

"In that case..."

Ducking forward, Barbara took him in her mouth. He closed his eyes and braced himself with one hand flat against the tile, the other cupped behind her head. Another moment and she found her rhythm, making Bolan grow with renewed desire.

She knew when he was ready, pulling back and turning off the shower as she rose. A towel was in her hand before he understood exactly what was happening.

"In bed this time."

The last time?

Bolan pushed the thought away and followed Barbara's lead. It didn't matter at the moment what tomorrow revealed. They had tonight, a sharing that his enemies could never take away.

Tomorrow would take care of itself.

Tonight the Executioner was standing down.

4

The church was small, constructed chiefly out of native stone and mortar and nearly overgrown with moss and creepers on the northern side. At one time, years ago, the padre had resented and resisted the encroachment of surrounding jungle on his church, but he no longer cared. If anything, it seemed the moss and creeping plants belonged exactly where they were, a living symbol of the church's melding with the land.

It had required some time for Father Julio Lazaro to decide the church wasn't his, after all. It was the house of God, and He permitted it to stand in service to His truth. When it had fully served its purpose, passed beyond its time, what better fate than reclamation by the forest and the soil?

From dust thou came. To dust thou shalt return.

The padre had been thinking frequently of dust during the past few weeks. It had begun with nagging pain inside, a now-and-then discomfort that was mostly *now,* until he called upon the doctor in Santa Rosa de Osos a few miles to the south. The tests were positive, their grim results confirmed upon examination by a specialist in Medellín.

Lazaro had six months to live, perhaps a year, if God was generous.

There had been options—chemotherapy and radiation treatments financed by the church—but it had seemed a waste. The padre felt death breathing down his neck, and he wasn't afraid. His faith, accumulated over time, prepared him for the mysteries ahead.

He worried most these days about his children in the forest. Father Lazaro's parish covered nearly a thousand square miles of mountainous jungle, spanning the major tributary of the Río Nechi, populated by a race of people who had changed little since the Europeans had first set foot upon the continent. Of course, they dressed in linen shirts and trousers now, with sandals on their feet—sometimes—and they occasionally trimmed their hair, but nothing else had really changed over the past five hundred years. His people still were children of the land, dependent on its bounty for survival, and they took their pleasure where they found it—often in the coca leaf.

Lazaro was a native of the district, and a man who kept himself informed. At fifty-seven he was old enough to recall La Violencia, the plague of human savagery that had descended on his homeland during 1948 and claimed at least two hundred thousand lives within the next ten years. La Violencia had been a major factor in Lazaro's ultimate decision to become a priest, and he'd praised God from the heart when the domestic slaughter seemed to taper off. Ten years of ceaseless killing, and the earth had drunk its fill of blood.

Until the *narcotraficantes* came. During the past ten years he'd been forced to watch as dealers, revolutionaries and reactionaries drenched his native land in blood again. The Indians he served were victimized in different ways—seduced to work the coca farms or hired as runners for the great cartels, coerced by armed guerrilla bands into supporting this or that political regime, assassinated if they failed to please their masters of the moment. When Lazaro pled his case before the authorities in Medellín and Bogotá, the men of power frowned and shook their heads, or simply turned away.

Of late he'd begun to pray for God to take a hand and save His children from their enemies. At first He hadn't answered, but the past few nights, Lazaro thought—imagined—that he felt a trembling in the earth, deep down, as if a giant had rolled over in his sleep.

Pure logic told him it was nothing but the common slippage of a fault line in the cordillera, possibly connected to the smoking mountain eight miles farther north. Except, he knew, the smoking mountain had been silent for a generation now.

He heard the vehicles approaching well before he saw them, recognized two engines and decided it wouldn't be soldiers or police. Around Lazaro's jungle parish soldiers left their camps in force or not at all, and the police would only stir outside their settlements if drawn by bribes or the report of some horrendous crime. In the past two weeks there had been nothing that would qualify; perhaps a dozen scattered homicides, involving mostly Indians, and they didn't concern police at all.

Not soldiers or police. Then who?

Guerrillas?

Terrorists?

He waited, relishing the feel of sunshine on his face, the heat that penetrated to his bones and made him warm as he was rarely warm these days. Whoever wanted him knew where he could be found seven days a week. He felt no apprehension or alarm at the approach of strangers; there was nothing they could do to him that fate hadn't already done.

The padre crossed his arms and waited in the sun outside God's house.

WHEN HE WAS just a child, Luis Costanza had seen his father carted off to prison on a murder charge. The victim, like his father, had been no one of importance in the scheme of things, so Juan Costanza had been sentenced to an "easy" term of thirty years instead of death before a military firing squad. He was assigned to serve his time in Bogotá at La Picata Prison, and he lasted all of eighteen months before an argument with other prisoners erupted into violence and he died from stab wounds in the prison yard.

These days his son knew La Picata as a house with a revolving door, but it required substantial cash and influence to have a prison term reduced, the doors thrown wide within a week or two of your arrival. Juan Costanza had been poor, a worthless cipher on the social scale, and one way or another he was meant to die inside the prison walls.

The lesson wasn't lost upon his son. Luis Costanza had grown up hating the authorities who had stolen his father's life, determined to evade their clutches and outwit them if he could. He wouldn't be a slave who worked for meager wages, living on the razor edge of hunger all his life, when it was easier to steal or smuggle contraband and live in style. He would use every trick at his disposal to avoid arrest, and failing that he would subvert the law with bribes or physically resist. If necessary, he would kill.

Growing up on the streets had been an education, of sorts. By the age of ten he'd been witness to a dozen murders in Medellín, the lesson sinking in that life was cheap, the richest man no more than fragile flesh and blood. He learned to handle weapons—poor antiques by modern standards, but they did the job—and he acquired a reputation as a lone wolf whom the older street thugs were advised to leave alone. At age fifteen he shot two men who tried to shake him down, and while they both survived, his reputation grew.

Luis Costanza was someone to respect . . . and fear.

He went to work for smugglers, hauling cigarettes, Scotch and transistors from Medellín to the northern ports of Barranquilla, Santa Marta, Ríohacha—anywhere, in short, where they could board a ship or aircraft bound for the United States. He was attacked en route from time to time, but he was never robbed. In three years he shot five men and made damn sure that none of them survived. On days when there was nothing headed north, he sometimes handled piecework as a bodyguard for older, more successful criminals. The next step, to become a hired assassin, was entirely logical. At twenty he had thirteen notches on his gun.

In North America, meanwhile, the so-called flower generation had discovered drugs. Their highest aspiration was to turn on and drop out of middle-class society, but someone had to help them get there, and the trip was never free of charge. Marijuana and cocaine, traditionally used by ghetto blacks and "hip" musicians, blossomed almost overnight into the drugs of choice among affluent Americans. The U.S. appetite for chemicals was insatiable, and if Colombian farmers couldn't produce enough coca leaves to satisfy the growing demand, ready supplies were available in Peru and Bolivia, imported for refinement at a string of mobile laboratories. Profits were incredible, and sudden millionaires began to formalize the structure of cartels in Medellín, in Bogotá and Calí, weeding out the competition as La Violencia returned to stay.

Luis Costanza began to cultivate associates among the very same authorities he'd despised in adolescence. They were still despicable—fat men in uniforms, expensive business suits or black judicial robes, all standing with their hands out—but they could be useful to a young man on the rise. He paid off jurists and attorneys, journalists and politicians, soldiers and police, remembering the guards at La Picata...just in case. Within a few short years Costanza had a private army at his beck and call, men like himself prepared to deal with enemies who didn't have a price.

Expansion into the United States had been a necessary risk. Costanza didn't trust his operation to the likes of Cuban boat-lift trash from Mariel or the Italians who enjoyed a virtual monopoly on trade in heroin. In fact, he trusted no one absolutely, but at least his own employees knew enough about the risk of cheating their employer that they generally kept their noses clean.

Miami was a problem from the start. There were so many Cubans on the scene already who believed the growing trade in drugs was theirs by right. It took a year of warfare on the streets to whip them into line, two more years for major dealers like Costanza and a number of his peers to kill or cow the small-time opposition drawn by whispers of the easy profits from cocaine. By 1982 the DEA and local law had logged 250 drug-related homicides around Miami, counting on perhaps an equal number they would never know about: dead bodies fed to alligators in the Everglades or white sharks in the Gulf of Mexico. When it was over, more or less, the market stabilized, and the men with badges almost seemed relieved.

The armistice produced a sudden glut of merchandise that cut the price of coke by half, and still the traffic flourished. Two good years, with nothing much to do but count the money that arrived and multiplied beyond the capabilities of any living man to spend it all. When stubborn justice minister Rodrigo Lara Bonilla rejected bribe offers in 1984 and declared his intention of driving the *narcotraficantes* out of business, his death sentence was handed down as a matter of course. Simple business in action.

And it was the worst mistake the cartel leaders ever made.

The government's reaction was immediate, with houses searched and jungle labs destroyed, hundreds of suspects jailed for interrogation and eventual trial. For the first time in decades extradition warrants from the United States were honored, even actively solicited. Costanza and a number of his peers were driven into exile, finding sanctuary in Panama City under the friendly wing of General Hector Caseros, but their every thought was turned toward going home.

Within a few short weeks Costanza and the others put out feelers to Colombia, establishing what journalists described as "narco-dialogue" in their attempt to find a common ground with angry politicians and police. The dealers offered to "retire" by slow degrees, an estimated ten-year plan with ample time for public indignation to subside, while government and private enterprise put on a show of rehabilitating native addicts, substituting crops, perhaps underwriting Colombia's heavy international debts. A television poll revealed that some forty-eight percent of the citizens consulted favored the plan, but Congress launched another witch hunt, playing for the headlines, and the deal went down in flames.

The rest, as someone reputedly said, was history. There were assassinations, bombings, endless threats, abductions, disappearances and full-scale battles in the streets. Two hundred court officials had been slaughtered in the past five years, with several thousand other homicides including journalists, attorneys, politicians and police, potential witnesses. A public declaration of war to the death was issued by ruthless men who called themselves "the Extraditables."

Costanza didn't care about the foreign press or world opinion. In his heart he knew the people of Colombia were on his side. They recognized the services he provided in the form of wages, charitable contributions—schools in Yarumal and Ambalema, hospitals in Quibdó and Aguadas—and suppression of the Communist guerrillas who were fond of picking new recruits at gunpoint from the mountain villages. Costanza's people loved him for his generosity, a trait they recognized as coming from the heart.

He meant to reinforce that sympathetic view today.

If only he could get that stubborn bastard of a priest to play along.

"YOU TELL HIM we were coming, boss?"

From the back seat of the new jeep Costanza could see the old priest waiting for them, like a scrawny figurine outside his ancient church.

"He must have heard us coming."

"He looks worn-out," the driver observed, his smile reflected in the rearview mirror. "They should trade in this old man for a priest with some balls."

"Priests don't need balls—" the shotgun rider said, and they both began to laugh.

"Shut up, the two of you," Costanza snapped, and there was instant silence in the car. "We've come to make this man of God our friend. You don't win friends with insults."

"Yes, sir."

Costanza didn't need to turn and check the second jeep as they pulled up outside the church. He knew it would be there, five soldiers armed and ready to respond the moment his life or liberty was threatened by his enemies.

Costanza waited for his driver to step out and open his door, all smiles as he emerged to greet the priest. The old man had rejected his initial overtures, a secondhand approach, but he'd never met Costanza or been subject to the dealer's charm.

All things were possible, Costanza thought, with cash in hand.

"Forgive the interruption, Father."

"I've been expecting you." The old man's eyes were like flint, his face a weathered parchment mask.

"I don't believe we've met," Costanza said.

"Your face is known to me from photographs. We sometimes read the papers even here."

"You're wise enough to know the press sometimes exaggerates."

"Sometimes." The priest was plainly not convinced.

"I wish to speak with you in private. May we step inside?"

"Your business has no place within the house of God."

Costanza felt the color rising in his cheeks. "What do you know about my business, Father?"

"All I need to know," the priest replied. "You deal in misery and death without regard for laws of God or man."

"A vicious slander spread by those who envy my success in business."

"Your success with *drugs*."

"A simple product of the land," Costanza countered. "Was it man who shaped the mountains? Who allows the coca leaf to grow? I deal in nature's bounty, nothing more."

"And kill in the defense of your unholy profits. Why not hand out scorpions to children in the village square as pets? At least their deaths would be swifter and more merciful."

Costanza felt his driver watching him, the others listening with windows down. They would expect him to react somehow, but he couldn't allow himself to strike a priest. Instead, he'd attempt to reach the man another way.

The dealer snapped his fingers, and his driver brought the satchel to him, fat with thousand-peso notes. Ten thousand dollars, more or less, in U.S. terms.

"Your church has need of various repairs," he said. "Perhaps a new home for your flock?"

"The church is strong enough, but I would tear it down myself before accepting help from those who trample on the sacred word of God."

Costanza felt his smile deserting him. He jerked the satchel open and displayed its contents. "With this your people may begin to educate and heal themselves. Would you deny them that?"

"Blood money," the priest scoffed. "No good can come of it."

Costanza stiffened, closed the satchel and returned it to his driver's waiting hands. "You're a stubborn man, but I admire your courage. It's a pity that your flock must suffer for an old man's ignorance and prejudice.''

"I won't have them further tainted by your sins."

"What have I done to make you hate me so?" Costanza asked, all wide-eyed innocence. "I give the people work and pay them wages out of all proportion to their worth. I build them schools and clinics to prolong their lives and help their children learn. Without the coca half of them would starve or end up begging in the streets of Medellín."

"A good Samaritan." The priest was almost sneering now. "And for your kindness all you seek is wealth beyond the wildest dreams of honest men, the power over life and death for those who would oppose your crimes."

"I love my country and her people, Father. Can you say the same?"

"This land is in disgrace because of you. Your poison jeopardizes every decent thing *my* country stands for. You corrupt the government, enslave the population with your drugs and murder those who dare to criticize."

Costanza felt the others staring at him, waiting. "If what you say is true, then you must be a hero . . . or a fool."

The priest regarded him with undisguised contempt. "I'm neither, just an old man coming to the end of his appointed time. I'm not frightened of your monkeys and their guns."

The driver made a move but stopped short when Costanza raised his hand. "The end of your appointed time draws closer, Father. You've hastened it today."

"Then do your worst," the priest replied. "I have no more to say."

With that he turned his back and retreated toward the ancient church. Costanza could have killed him with a nod, a gesture of his hand, but he wouldn't allow himself the luxury. There was no victory in murdering a shriveled priest when you could find a way to make him crawl and beg instead.

"We go!" he snapped, the driver blinking once before he caught the door and held it for his master. None of them quite understood why the priest was still alive.

Another time perhaps.

And in the meantime Costanza would find a way to let the old man's parishioners know why their church was old and crumbling, hymn books tattered with the pages falling out. The word of his attempted generosity would spread, the foolish priest's rejection offered in a different light for thinking men to recognize and understand.

When the old man was ready to apologize, Costanza might forgive him.

Possibly.

The day it snowed in hell.

5

"Heads up."

Mack Bolan felt a sudden flash of déjà vu, its origins not difficult to trace—another flight with Jack Grimaldi, and another private airfield, their arrival timed precisely to avoid a storm of hostile antiaircraft fire. For something like a heartbeat he was back at Stony Man, expecting Brognola, Barbara Price and the rest of them to meet him on the ground, before his mind clicked into the here and now.

Colombia's northernmost point was the Guajira Peninsula, thrust into the Caribbean like a beckoning finger, pointing toward the Netherlands Antilles. On the east, man's boundary coincided with nature's in the form of the Sierra de Perijá, a clear dividing line between Colombia and Venezuela.

Guajira was a curious amalgam of Chicago under Al Capone and the Wild West. While most Colombian narcotics were refined and manufactured in the "Cocaine Triangle"—with anchor points at Calí, Medellín and Bogotá—the exportation was a different game. With open war declared and narcoterrorism making daily headlines all around the world, security and customs searches at the major airports had compelled the drug lords to revise their strategies and find new outlets for *la merca,* the merchandise. The result was the creation of a lawless no-man's-land dotted with armed camps and private airfields. The ports of Santa Marta and Ríohacha offered alternative points of departure for shipments to Miami and New Orleans, but light aircraft remained the most popular means of transport.

The cartels had their own protected airfields—under constant guard—but in the past few years the traffic in cocaine had grown by leaps and bounds, with independent traders horning in wherever possible. It made no difference to the narcobarons, in the end; they satisfied the standing orders from their stateside buyers, stepping up production where they could to meet demand, and on the side they sold their surplus to the independents—"cocaine cowboys" who would risk a night flight off the coast of Cuba, skimming ten or fifteen feet above the waves to outwit Castro's radar teams.

Before the independents had a chance to buy *la merca,* though, they had to land, and so a string of "open" airstrips had been bulldozed in the rocky soil of La Guajira. They were "open" in the sense that independent pilots were allowed to land and leave again, provided they paid the going rate, but there was standard protocol to be observed. Initial contact was required through trusted intermediaries, with specific dates and ETAs assigned. As in the case of Stony Man, an uninvited drop-in could provoke immediate attack.

"They call this pit stop Libertad," Grimaldi said. "As in life, liberty and the pursuit of nose candy."

"As long as we're cleared to land."

"No sweat. Between us, Hal and I came up with all the necessary references. You ever stop and think he's got some sleazy friends?"

"It crossed my mind."

The choice of La Guajira was a natural, all things considered. With a doctored passport Bolan could have easily flown into Bogotá or Medellín, but they were packing heavy ordnance in Grimaldi's twin-engine Beechcraft, and that kind of load couldn't clear customs. The private strips, conversely, took your cash and topped your fuel tanks off, no questions asked. Between arrival and departure you were under guard—for both your own protection and the strip's security—but no one gave a damn where you were going when you left, or what you might be hauling in the cargo hold.

The strip was long and narrow, sprouting grass and weeds, which the proprietors encouraged. It cultivated the appearance of an airfield long abandoned and out of use. Another plane and several vehicles were tucked away beneath the cover of some nearby trees, with netting strung to aid the camouflage. The fuel tank, masquerading as a rusty water tower, stood beside an ancient barn that might have crumbled at a hearty sneeze.

"Nice place."

Grimaldi flashed a smile. "You ought to see the rooms they rent."

"I'll pass."

"No sense of romance, that's your problem."

"Not today."

The welcoming committee was composed of three mestizos. One of them approached the Beechcraft to accept Grimaldi's cash and fuel the plane. His partners carried automatic weapons, and they lingered by the barn some thirty feet apart, prepared to rake the new arrivals with a deadly cross fire if there was a deviation from the script. As Bolan stretched his legs, he checked the tree line and spotted two more gunners hidden there.

It was a decent system, and he knew they could have been in trouble if they tried to crash the party, unannounced. The odds weren't bad, once you were on the ground, but taking off or landing under hostile fire would be difficult.

Gassing up took the better part of fifteen minutes, and Bolan was ready when Grimaldi called him back. Phase one would be complete when they had lifted off and aimed the Beechcraft toward Medellín.

Two hours, give or take," Grimaldi reported.

"Okay."

"I'm wondering, is this trip really necessary?"

"Bet your life."

Grimaldi wore a rueful smile as he replied, "Too late."

AN ESTIMATED 1.7 million people lived in Medellín, the capital of Antioquia Province and the second-largest city in Colombia. The locals called themselves *paisas,* and were an aggressive and ambitious people with an eye for "easy" profits, unintimidated by the risks involved. The ruling class in Bogotá traditionally looked upon *paisas* with disdain, dismissing them as peasants and the butt of countless jokes. But by the 1960s Medellín had turned the joke around.

Downtown the city bustled with traffic, skyscrapers towering above the mile-high river valley and pine forests of north-central Antioquia. Stately colonial homes shared space with three universities, botanical gardens and dozens of parks. Tree-lined boulevards gave way to winding roads in the suburban hills, where affluent *paisas* kept their spacious country homes and weekend chalets. A little farther and the tourist would discover neat white stucco farmhouses, sporting crimson trim and flower boxes overhanging tidy patios.

Behind its picturesque facade, however, life was hard—and often short—in Medellín. With a population one-fifth the size of New York City, Medellín still managed a yearly per capita homicide rate ten times that of the crime-ridden Big Apple. Seventy percent of the victims slaughtered in 1989 fell between the ages of fourteen and nineteen years, effectively decimating the next generation of Colombian youth.

Nervous cabdrivers habitually locked their doors after picking up a fare in Colombia's second city, the better to guard against *gamines*—mobile wolf packs of children as young as nine who cruised the streets around the clock in search of prey. Beyond the city limits Antioquia and the surrounding provinces had been divided into independent fiefdoms ruled by right-wing death squads, Stalinist guerrilla factions and the mercenary barons of cocaine.

Ironically the affluence of Medellín and its oppressive plague of violent crime both shared a common source. Drug profits lay behind a large percentage of the city's growth, with more than half of the population listed as employed in service occupations, catering to tourists—few and far between these days—and to the wealthy locals who secured their fortunes from the land. In Antioquia Province that meant coffee or cocaine, and sometimes both, the growers branching out from one crop to the other as they realized that greater profits were available outside the law.

The Executioner had come to Medellín without a detailed battle plan, deliberately remaining flexible. He meant to take advantage of the strained relationship between Costanza and his chief competitors, but he hadn't selected concrete targets prior to touchdown at the scene.

One thing was certain: there wouldn't be any shortage of potential marks. The drug lords had invested widely, everything from real estate to banking and insurance firms, in addition to more traditional pursuits like gambling, prostitution and pornography. A ghoulish twist in recent years had been the traffic in black market blood, a medical commodity in short supply from Guatemala to the major hospitals of Bogotá. While he wasn't prepared to credit tales of "blood farms" in the jungle, Bolan knew that plasma shipments had been hijacked, held for ransom, sometimes switched in secret for the tainted blood of derelicts and native tribesmen riddled with disease.

Too many starting places, and he wasn't prepared to launch his local hit-and-run campaign with a direct assault against Costanza or his peers. Despite Brognola's deadline, he was looking forward to a game of cat and mouse—

or hide-and-seek—in which his enemies would play a crucial role. It would be Bolan's job to get them started, sniping back and forth at one another, and to make sure no one from the list of heavy players walked away when it was done. Between times there was ample room for flexibility, and he was content to let the savages destroy one another, if they would.

The list of targets Brognola had wheedled out of the DEA was too damn long for Bolan to attempt them all, but he was free to pick and choose for maximum effect. He made the first selection almost totally at random, counting on the general atmosphere of violence and confusion in Colombia to cover his initial tracks, diverting the suspicion of his chosen mark toward well-known enemies.

It was a gamble, but the Executioner felt confident in his selection. Confident enough, in fact, that he would take it to the bank.

RAUL RODRIGUEZ WAS the smallest of Colombia's "Big Three" cocaine suppliers, both in stature—five foot two without his lifts—and in the size of his illicit empire. His yearly income peaked somewhere around five hundred million dollars during 1989, and revenue for 1990 was expected to improve by close to twenty-five percent. It was more cash than most men could expect to see, much less possess, within a lifetime, but the harvest didn't stop him wanting more.

For openers, Rodriguez had desired to keep his money safe and make it "clean." The answer was simplicity itself, and in the spring of 1986 he had acquired a bank to call his own. The president and officers were all legitimate, within the understanding of that term in Medellín, which meant they readily agreed to launder the illegal profits from cocaine, recycle them as loans or straight investment into high-yield bonds and help Rodriguez multiply his loot in relative security. The record of deposits was revised to indicate Rodriguez earned his keep from coffee and petroleum, while funnelling his profits into real estate, construction and the import-export trade.

The latter was correct, at least, and while outstanding extradition warrants kept Rodriguez from impulsive visits to the bank, his influence was felt in every move the president and his directors made.

It was a start, and Bolan viewed it as a challenge, something rather different from the standard smash-and-grab he'd employed for years against the stateside Mafia.

The president was waiting in his spacious office for Bolan when he arrived, dressed up for the occasion in a thousand-dollar suit and Gucci loafers. The warrior also carried a large attaché case and looked every inch the wealthy businessman he was supposed to be. The actual appointment had been easy to arrange, once Bolan started quoting numbers for deposit in his new account. It was only proper for the president to greet a new depositor who promised quarterly investments in the fifteen-million-dollar range.

"Good afternoon, Señor Belasko. I'm Carlos Molina. May I be among the first to welcome you to Medellín?"

"I'm looking forward to a profitable stay."

"Of course. If we can be of help to you at any time..."

"My first concern is with security. I'm sure you understand."

"A wise man always takes precautions."

"I'm impressed with what I've heard about your bank from friends in the United States—"

"You're are too kind."

"But I believe in double-checking everything myself."

"I understand."

"The vault, for instance."

"Ah."

"I know it's an unusual request, but I'd appreciate a look around, to satisfy my curiosity, you might say."

Molina didn't appear surprised. It figured that the type of men he normally did business with would be suspicious, checking every angle to make sure their loot was safe before they placed it in another's hands.

"Allow me to conduct you on a tour."

The smaller man was on his feet and moving, even as he spoke, a human dynamo in the pursuit of waiting cash. They caught the elevator several paces from his office and rode it down. Molina retrieved a set of keys from one of his assistants and opened the metal grate that barred access to the vault. The main door—three feet thick and solid steel, complete with time lock and alarms—stood open during business hours, granting ready access to the safe-deposit boxes and reserve of cash inside.

"It looks impressive," Bolan remarked as he was shown around the cool interior.

"We have the latest in security devices, cameras and alarms, as well as the guards you saw outside."

"Okay, I'm sold. There's only one more thing..."

"Yes, sir?"

He handed the attaché case to Molina and smile. "Fill it up."

"I beg your pardon?"

"The Rodriguez box. I'm interested in U.S. currency, no pesos."

The president returned his smile. "A joke, surely."

"Not quite."

The Beretta changed Molina's mind. He began to sputter, going pale. "To open a deposit box without the patron's key is quite impossible," he said. "Security—"

"Is never perfect," Bolan finished for him, leveling the automatic at his chest. "I know you have a way to crack the box in case a key gets lost. We'll just pretend."

"But what you ask—"

"I didn't ask. I'm telling you to let me see the box, or we can say goodbye right now, and I'll do business with your second-in-command."

"You can't expect to get away with this."

"My problem. Yours is filling up the bag and making sure you don't miss anything."

Reluctantly the president led Bolan to a row of boxes in the eastern corner of the vault. He used a key from his assistant's ring, then drew a master from his own vest pocket to complete the turn. The box was heavy, and a glance inside showed deeds and stock certificates, as well as bundled cash.

It was too much for Bolan's briefcase to accommodate, so he stuffed several extra bundles into his pockets, making sure they didn't bulge enough to make him look suspicious on the long walk back.

"Don't close it," Bolan ordered. He holstered the Beretta, palmed an incendiary stick, then dropped it in the box on top of the remaining bundles of thousand-dollar bills.

"What are you doing?"

"Turning up the heat. Let's go—and play it cool around the guards, unless your wife looks good in black."

They had another thirty seconds to go before ignition, and they made it to the elevator, Bolan watching Molina for any signal to his staff. The elevator doors were sliding shut before one teller caught a whiff of smoke from the direction of the vault and started back to check it out.

The warrior punched a button for the seventh floor and prodded the banker ahead of him until they reached the service stairs, with access to the roof. As they emerged in sunlight, Molina was obviously puzzled, certain there could be no exit for this madman, short of leaping to his death.

They heard the helicopter simultaneously, half a minute later, closing from the south. Grimaldi circled once and hovered overhead before he set it down, the rotor wash unseating the banker's toupee and skimming it across the

"Once more around the park," Bolan directed, opening the briefcase on his lap and staring at the money for a moment.

"You're sure?"

"I'm sure."

Bolan started to rip through the paper bands that held each wad of thousand-dollar bills. As each in turn was free, he tossed it out the open hatch beside him, watched it blow away like green confetti, drifting toward the busy streets below.

"Your buddy's going to bust a gut, you know that?"

"I'm counting on it, Jack."

"You've got a crazy way of making friends."

"With some guys you have to get their full attention first."

"I guess you've got that down, all right."

"We'll see."

"They get you on the cameras going in?"

"For what it's worth. He's bound to blame Costanza for the grab, no matter who he sees on tape."

Grimaldi pointed them downtown, the trail of money playing out as Bolan finished dumping the attaché case. He kept the hundred thousand dollars in his pockets, waiting for a chance to spend it on the demolition of his enemies.

"I guess we're in it now," Grimaldi said.

"You could say that."

And both of them began to chuckle, laughing in the face of death.

6

McCarter was the odd man out, and that was fine. There were three Spanish-speakers on the team, which meant that Katz and Gary Manning had to double up with Calvin James and Rafael Encizo when they hit the streets.

So far, so good.

The Briton wasn't afraid of working solo. He'd done this kind of job before, on other turf, and it was all the same if you maintained perspective, watching out for unexpected moves and enemies you hadn't counted on in the beginning. Anything was fair if it produced results and let the good guys walk away intact.

First up, their mission was to find out who the good guys were.

He lit a cigarette and scanned the street in each direction. The signs of last year's coup attempt against "beloved" President Caseros had been more or less erased, but a few reminders of the violence lingered on. Across the street, high up beneath the eaves of a boutique, he saw the telltale pockmarks left by automatic gunfire. A careless burst, perhaps the last defiant gesture of a dying man.

The posters were more prominent—Caseros in his uniform, resplendent, smiling down upon his subjects like a chunky Latin version of Orwell's Big Brother.

Hermano grande.

But the bastard didn't look so *grande,* even with his braided cap and service ribbons, medals he awarded to himself from time to time in recognition of his "service to the people." Take the uniform away and you'd have another grubby Third World strongman, neck-deep in corruption and supported by the underlings who stood to profit while he held the reins of government.

McCarter's job on day one of the Panama campaign was to connect with one of Washington's surviving friends on the Caseros military team. His name was Pablo Arevalo, and he held the rank of captain in the infantry. McCarter wasn't sure precisely how he had survived the coup attempt of 1989, but that was history in any case. Unless...

Unless the captain was a ringer, planted by Caseros to ingratiate himself with the Americans and keep his boss informed of any future U.S. moves in Panama.

Would Langley recognize a double in the desperate rush to dig up allies, *any* allies, on the troubled isthmus? Would controllers stop and check their source, or would they simply pass him on as someone to be trusted in a crunch?

It was a point to ponder as he crossed the street and spent a few more minutes window-shopping, finally satisfied that he hadn't been tailed from his hotel. Of course, if Arevalo was a double, then a tail would be superfluous, a waste of time. Caseros merely had to wait and read the transcript of their conversation when he had the time.

McCarter didn't want to think that he'd been betrayed so early in the game, but he'd stayed alive this long by verifying each and every covert contact for himself. One bright spot, either way it played, was that the captain would be ignorant of Phoenix Force and their specific mission in the capital of Panama. As far as Arevalo knew, he was supposed to meet one man and share his knowledge of the local drug trade, nothing more. McCarter meant to let it rest at that until he had a private reading on the man's dependability.

The bar was dark and loud inside, the kind of place where "hostesses" waited at the door to seat male customers and offer them companionship as long as they kept buying drinks. The rest of it was optional, depending on the patron's needs and willingness to pay, and there were rooms upstairs to keep the hostesses from straying with the house's cut.

McCarter let a slender young-old woman lead him to a corner table, stopping her before she had a chance to sit and plant a warm hand on his thigh. If looks could kill, he'd have been a dead man on the spot, but he was in, prepared to wait, with a commanding view of what appeared to be the only entrance from the street.

A barmaid brought him watered beer, and McCarter sipped at it while he waited, checking out the crowd. A third-rate band was going through its repertoire on stage, a sorry blend of salsa and frenetic heavy metal that came out sounding like the racket from a foundry.

"Is this seat taken?"

Arevalo stood there, as big as life, half shouting to be heard above the band. He wasn't in uniform, but the man matched the snapshots McCarter had seen at Stony Man the day before.

He nodded toward the empty chair, and Arevalo hooked it closer so that they wouldn't have to scream at each other.

"Señor McGill?"

It was the name imprinted on McCarter's bogus passport, and he nodded. "Captain."

"Call me Pablo, please."

"I want to thank you for your help."

"I've done nothing yet."

McCarter did his best to make his smile sincere. "I'm confident you will. Should we adjourn to some more private place?"

"Upstairs," Arevalo replied. "I've made arrangements for a room."

"Lead on."

He trailed a yard or two behind the captain, grateful for the weight of his Beretta 92-F in its shoulder sling beneath the lightweight jacket that he wore. If Arevalo was about to spring a trap, McCarter had a few tricks of his own in store.

The room was small, more like a walk-in closet, and furnished with a folding table and a pair of mismatched chairs. A muffled echo of the band reverberated through the floorboards as they sat down facing each other.

Captain Arevalo broke the ice. "You wish to speak of drugs?"

"Cocaine, specifically."

McCarter didn't know if they were wired for sound, but it would make no difference if he played his role and let his contact do the talking.

"Many shipments stop here on their way to the United States. Our president deals with some of the Colombians directly. For a price they're allowed to hide in Panama from time to time. A few have homes outside the city, where they visit several times each year. Safe conduct for the dealers and their poison has been guaranteed. Caseros has the army at their beck and call."

"I've heard all this before. The problem is, I need hard evidence."

"And if you had such proof?"

McCarter shrugged. "Then I go back and weigh my options, figure out the best approach for getting what we both desire."

The captain frowned. "And what is that?"

"Perhaps, if you told me . . ."

"I wish to see the honor of my native land restored. Caseros and his *putas* are a national disgrace. He must be forcibly deposed while there is still a country left for us to save."

"As bad as that?"

"The Communists are gaining strength each day because so many peasants hate Caseros and believe the United States is powerless to root him out. I fear a revolution if the patriots among us don't find a way to purge this cancer from the land."

"Speaking of purges, I'm a bit surprised to find you still in uniform, the way you feel about your president."

"I was assigned to hunt guerrillas west of Santiago when the coup began. There was no time for me to move against the capital."

"Things happen," McCarter said, trying hard to read the captain's eyes. He had a hunch that Arevalo was sincere, but he wasn't prepared to let his guard down yet.

"You mentioned proof."

"That's right. Not hearsay, or what someone claims he saw. Hard proof's the only thing that I can use right now."

"Like photographs? Caseros with his friends from Medellín perhaps? A tape recording of their conversation?"

It was McCarter's turn to frown. "Such tapes and photographs exist?"

"Perhaps. If we should meet again . . ."

"I'm counting on it, Pablo."

"I'd need assurances from those you represent."

"Such as?"

"Consideration for my services when Caseros is deposed."

"I don't forget my friends."

The captain eyed him for a moment, and finally allowed himself a cautious smile. "Remain at your hotel. I'll be in touch."

"Don't wait too long. I'm working on a deadline here."

"Tomorrow or the next day at the latest."

"Very well."

"I leave you now. Five minutes, *sí?*"

McCarter nodded and remained where he was as the captain left the room. Slowly he relaxed—not totally convinced, by any means, but fairly certain there'd be no ambush waiting for him on the stairs or in the bar. If Arevalo had intended something rash, he'd have dropped the net before instead of walking out to leave a job undone.

Hard evidence.

If true, it was a portion of the break they had been looking for, a chance to undermine Caseros and expose his skein of lies.

THE NIGHTCLUB had been fingered as a local smugglers' paradise, a place where deals where closed and drops arranged. A raid wouldn't have turned up drugs in any major quantity, but if you knew who you were looking for, it might be possible to watch the dealers as they went about their business, talking megabucks and kilos underneath the colored lights. The dance band turned out easy Latin rhythms, breaking every forty minutes with a deejay standing by.

"I was expecting more," Gary Manning said, sipping his rum and cola. "We have a hundred bars like this in Montreal."

Across the table Calvin James put on a sour face. "Your basic dealer's notion of a place with class is strobes and lots of noise. They never got the word that disco's dead, I guess."

"Are we expecting anyone?"

"Potluck. You never know the way these bastards move around. One day they're playing with themselves in Medellín, next thing you know they're in Miami or New York."

"Or Panama?"

"Let's keep our fingers crossed."

"I have a feeling we're going into this the long way around."

"Whatever. If it works, we've got the chance to put a couple of heavy mothers out of business, maybe crimp the cartel's style. In my book that's worth the wait."

"My point is," Manning countered, "we could sit in clubs like this the next ten days and never see a thing."

"Or we could hit right off," the black man answered, smiling. "Take a look down there, third table from the stage."

The profile could have been a look-alike, but then their pigeon turned around to flag a cocktail waitress, and they both knew there was no mistake.

"Mercado," Manning said.

"The very same."

"Somebody up there likes us, Cal."

"Or maybe they're just sick of *him*."

"I'll second that."

"Be cool. We haven't got the green to tag this scumbag yet. Enjoy your drink. We'll baby-sit, and maybe later we can see him home."

"I still say it's the long way around."

James smiled, his eyes fixed on José Mercado as he sipped his beer.

"Sometimes," he said, "it takes a while to do things right."

"WE'RE BEING followed," Rafael Encizo announced.

"I made them," Katz replied. "Two right behind and three across the street."

"They look like children."

Katzenelenbogen took his time and dawdled past the lighted window of a jewelry shop, ignoring several prostitutes who stood nearby, appraising him.

"You never know."

"You want to shake them?"

"Let's see what happens. If they haven't made a move within the next few minutes, we can always hail a cab."

They'd been checking out the streets since dusk with no real destination fixed in mind. A wise man got to know his battleground before he started a war, and Katz believed in taking full advantage of terrain. In this case they were operating in what had to be considered hostile territory, veering toward a collision course with the established military government, and any slip along the way could get them killed.

The Auerbach connection worried him the most, and at the same time it was infuriating. He remembered Isaac Auerbach as a "can-do" infantry commander, the type who never sent his men ahead when he could lead. The wounds he'd suffered in the Six Day War weren't debilitating, but Auerbach had come out of the hospital with his remaining eye set firmly on a new career. Mossad had been the answer, and they'd worked together half a dozen times on different projects, hunting terrorists or running agents in the occupied territories. Though never close to Auerbach, Katz remembered him as being somewhat cold, aloof and distant, not at all the sort expected to spark charismatic loyalty and commitment in a group of combat soldiers.

Still, war changed men, and damn near getting killed could provoke the biggest change of all. In some it caused striking alterations in perspective: misers started to throw their cash around as if it was going out of style; a ladies' man might find himself reduced to impotence; a kind man might turn hard and cruel.

Katz didn't like to speculate on the psychology of men he never really knew, but he'd heard enough to know that Auerbach was separated from Mossad for murdering an Arab prisoner. The shooting, in and of itself, might not have been enough to drive him out—such things had certainly been swept beneath the rug before, and would again—but Auerbach refused to sign the usual pro forma reprimand. Instead, he bucked the ranking brass, insisting that his action be approved, the blot upon his record instantly erased. The end result had been a quiet backdoor exit into private enterprise, Trans-Global sprouting up to serve the needs of frightened businessmen around Jerusalem and Tel Aviv, eventually branching out as other war zones beckoned with the smell of blood and money.

After all of that it still surprised Katz to discover that Auerbach was working for the drug lords.

There were three young men behind them now, communicating with their partners on the far side of the street by means of looks and hand signs. Six on two, but Katz wasn't tremendously concerned about the odds unless the boys were packing heat. With empty hands or knives and bludgeons, the odds wouldn't be a problem. Katz held a black belt in karate, while Encizo studied both karate and kung fu. If it came down to killing, both of them had knives and pistols.

Simple, right.

Unless the boys were something more than simple muggers. In the troubled Latin countries, Katzenelenbogen knew, assassins came in every shape and size, but teenage youths were favorites of the underworld and various guerrilla movements, with their look of innocence and knowledge of the streets in cities where they lived. A youthful beggar or a shoeshine boy drew scant attention in a crowd, and he could wield a blade or pull a trigger in the time it took a victim to decide he was at risk. It was a brand-new age of opportunity for Third World teens—the chance to prove yourself a man by spilling blood for money.

Katz knew that he was borrowing trouble, projecting worst-case scenarios, and he concentrated on the street, Encizo at his side, both men alert and searching for strategic ground.

"The alley?" Encizo suggested.

It was just ahead of them and on the right, dark enough to offer them some privacy if things got rough.

"All right," Katz replied.

They made as if to pass it by, then veered hard right and disappeared before their six pursuers had a chance to think, straight on, along the alley to a midway point where they could see the lights and watch the traffic flow on either side.

The two men stopped to wait.

It took a moment for the boys to get there, and Katz pictured frantic gestures, beckoning their backup from the wrong side of the street. They huddled to decide their strategy, then Katz saw them coming down the alley three abreast. One of them bent to pick a scrap of wood off the ground.

"They want to play," Encizo said.

"Their game, our rules."

The young men wasted no time on preliminaries. As they came within striking range, two rushed directly into the attack, the others trying to surround their prey and cut off retreat. It obviously hadn't crossed their minds that Katz and Encizo had picked the alley on their own, that they were standing fast.

The first youth in was tall and slender, with dirty hair and denims. He swung a length of chain without considering his target. Katz took it on his prosthetic arm and stepped close, inside the blow, to hammer open ribs with a destructive left. The young man folded, leaving the Israeli the chain as he collapsed.

Encizo used a roundhouse kick to empty his assailant's knife hand, feinting to the left, then bringing up his right foot in a snap that pushed the blademan's lower jaw an inch off-line and dropped him in his tracks. If he survived the night, the guy would be on liquid diets for the next few weeks.

More blades, the closest one on Katz's right and bearing in. He whipped around the chain and snared the young attacker's wrist, numb fingers opening to drop the knife as his assailant yelped in pain. Before the hoodlum could retreat, Katz caught him with a one-two elbow back and forth across the face. A spurt of crimson burst from the flattened nose. He was reeling when a raking kick across his left knee finished it.

Three were down, and Katz turned in time to see Encizo finish numbers four and five. The attackers had finally grasped the fact that one-on-one was going nowhere fast, but they'd left the job too long. Blades flashing, two of them rushed Encizo, cursing, and the Cuban scuttled back a pace to make them overshoot their mark. It was the edge he needed. He ducked beneath a thrust and caught his nearer adversary by the gonads, swinging him around to let him take the second blade.

It might not be a mortal wound—at least the guy was moving when he fell—but the surprise of scoring on a teammate left Encizo's second target gaping, open for the kick that nearly took his head off.

The last attacker broke and ran, machismo flying out the window in a heartbeat as he saw his comrades lying on the ground. Encizo called an insult after him in Spanish, but the runner had already seen and heard enough. He disappeared without a backward glance and left his two intended victims standing in the littered alleyway, with five men down.

"Can anybody talk?" Katz asked.

"This one, I think."

Encizo knelt beside the boy who'd been stabbed and gripped his cheek, twisting flesh until the eyes popped open and he was rewarded with a bleat of pain. He started firing questions off in Spanish.

"Dinero."

Money.

"Shit."

The attack had been a simple mugging, and it put them nowhere close to Auerbach or Feldman. They'd have to keep on trolling, working the informants Brognola had managed to supply and hope that something broke before their time ran out.

7

"One thing I want to know, is how come you always get the girl?"

Carl Lyons glanced at Rosario Blancanales and grinned. "Hey, what can I tell you, Pol? It's karma. Anyway, you're next on tap in case she likes the fatherly approach."

"I've got your fatherly approach, right here."

They sat in Hermann Schwarz's room, an eighth-floor beachfront suite in a hotel on Bayshore Drive. Gadgets stood at the sliding doors, studying the ocean view. "Time out," he said at last. "Before we write another comedy routine, let's make damn sure we've got our act together where it counts."

"It's cool," Lyons said.

"Humor me, okay?"

Lyons shrugged. "Okay, I've got a two o'clock with this Maria Teresina at her place on Seventeenth. I keep the date and find out what she knows about Costanza's action in Miami."

"Right. With all the flak she's taking on her antidrug campaign, she ought to have a fix on who's in charge. With any luck we just might get a handle on this Spider character."

"Good luck," Blancanales said. "If she knew the guy, she would've turned him in to the police, like she did those other dealers."

"Not necessarily. The other times she had enough to make it stick in court. There might be something in the way of street talk, or she could be covering for an informant in the gang."

"Don't hold your breath."

"It's worth a shot." Lyons glanced at his watch to verify he still had forty minutes before the scheduled rendezvous.

In fact, it might turn out to be their only shot. With so many dealers in Miami and environs, weeding out Costanza's people—much less the elusive killer known as La Araña—could have taken them a month. Instead, they had only ten days in which to do their job, and one of those half gone. Maria Teresina was their last, best hope of cutting through the bureaucratic bull, red tape and phony leads, to find what they were looking for and nail it down before their time ran out.

During the past eleven months, the woman had become a heroine of sorts around Miami, opening a storefront office to attack the cocaine cowboys one-on-one. She dealt with addicts and their families, directing users into rehabilitation programs and collecting cash to keep them there until the cure stuck. Whenever possible she also gathered evidence against the dealers—everything from snapshots and videos of curbside deals to affidavits from the users she had turned around. The evidence was delivered to Metro-Dade and the DEA for prosecution in the courts. At first her progress has embarrassed the police, but they'd gotten over it. To date the D.A.'s office gave Maria Teresina credit for convictions on three middleweights and ten or fifteen runners who were either serving time or sweating out appeals.

Which gave the lady mixed reviews, to start with. Cameras loved her, and the newshawks ate it up, with feature spots and interviews each time her efforts brought another dealer down. She'd received awards for public service from a dozen civic groups, and various foundations had been taking turns on rent to keep the storefront open and available.

The flip side was a different story, though. It seemed the dealers and a number of their clientele resented the publicity, felony indictments and jail time. There had been threats, and vandals had attacked her office half a dozen times, with damage ranging from a broken window to a flash fire that had necessitated a total overhaul. The landlord had considered eviction, in the latter case, but warnings out of city hall had wised him up. He had decided it would be the decent thing to donate labor and materials instead.

And there were death threats.

"You're with the DEA, remember," Blancanales said. "A special operator out of Washington."

"No sweat."

"Hal's got the number covered if she tries to check it out."

"I know that, Pol."

"Okay. Meanwhile, I'm working on Costanza's competition. It's a long shot, but if anybody's got a fix on La Araña, I'll put money on the opposition. They'll be motivated, anyway."

"It hasn't done them any good so far," Schwarz said. "Two dozen hits in the past six months on dealers working for Mercado and Rodriguez. They could use a course in self-defense."

"Too bad we can't sit back and let them take each other out," Lyons commented.

"I'd buy it if they weren't so frigging careless."

"Right."

The same six months had seen eleven innocent civilians killed or wounded in a string of drive-by shootings that had snuffed out twenty-five Mercado and Rodriguez soldiers in Dade and Broward counties. The MO of the assassins had become familiar to police: a motorcycle weaving in and out of traffic, jumping lights, their automatic weapons raking anyone who stood within a dozen paces of the human target. They were *sicarios,* and this time they were leaving trails of blood on U.S. soil.

"I'd still feel better if we had some kind of linkup with the others," Schwarz remarked. "Coordinate the moves, you know?"

"We're stuck with what we've got," Lyons replied. "Mack and Phoenix have got problems of their own. The best thing we can do is wrap our end up fast and disengage."

"Suits me," Politician said. "I don't care much for standing in reserve."

"We run the Spider down, I figure we'll be playing with the first string all the way."

"You promise?"

"Have I ever let you down?" Ironman asked.

"Well, since you mention it—"

"Let's get our act into gear," Schwarz said. "The opposition isn't taking any breathers, and we're far enough behind the game as it is."

"I hear you, Coach."

"Hear this. They're counting on our play to starve Costanza out. Cut off his distribution—even make a decent start—and he goes back to living on his cash reserves. An army has to eat, and Striker will be needing all the help we can give him."

"Say no more. I'm on my way."

"And one more thing," Gadgets added. "Let's be careful out there, hmm?"

"I'm tired of being careful," Lyons replied. "Why don't we kick some ass?"

Schwarz flashed a crooked smile. "That, too."

THE STOREFRONT OFFICE stood on southwest Seventeenth, two blocks from Shenandoah Park. The sun was warm against Carl Lyons's face as he took time to scan the street, discovering no trace of the police or hostile eyes.

And how much difference, Lyons wondered, would there really be between the two?

He knew damn well that some Miami cops resented any citizen who grabbed a headline fighting crime and thereby made the force seem less efficient—even criminally negligent. It was the same from coast to coast wherever narcs and street cops got together, putting down the "goody two-shoes" who had nerve enough to meddle in "police affairs." In some places that had changed a bit over the past few years, with television shows encouraging Joe Average to report the whereabouts of wanted felons, but the attitude was still pervasive anywhere you looked.

Civilians were supposed to take their licks and cut their losses, call the cops and wait for word. They were supposed to wait forever and keep their mouths shut in the meantime, if so ordered by a badge.

Times change, and they were changing in Miami. Citizens were getting over their initial shock at the cocaine wars, shaking off their apathy as trouble started creeping closer to their homes and endangering their families. They didn't want to hear that there was nothing anyone could do about the plague of drugs.

Maria Teresina got out on the street, or showed up on TV, and she wasn't afraid to look the average citizen in the eye. She told him things were bad and getting worse, in case he didn't know, but there was something he could do about it . . . if he had the nerve. He and his friends could start to gather evidence against their local dealers, snapping photographs and making buys with witnesses on hand, recording conversations, noting license numbers—and they could deliver the material to prosecutors with demands for action. If the D.A. failed to move, Maria and her home-grown media machine were standing by to turn up the heat, raising questions of incompetence or possible complicity that opposition candidates were bound to resurrect around election time. If dealers walked, she told the people, their elected prosecutors should prepare to do the same.

There had been two attempts to roust her in the past few months that Lyons knew about—once over parking violations on the street outside her office, and a second rap—more serious—involving the possession of cocaine. The latter charge had fallen flat when she produced a video recording of the buy and named the dealer as a Metro-Dade detective's son. Since then, hands-off had been the game, but you could never tell when someone might decide to take another stab at plucking this attractive thorn from the department's flesh.

Assuming, always, that the dealers didn't tag her first.

The office had no air-conditioning, but they were getting by with giant floor fans mounted in opposite corners of the room. They made more noise than difference, and an electric typewriter was contributing its share, along with ringing phones. The young secretary smiled and raised an index finger, asking him to wait while she took the call.

"Miami TIP. We turn in pushers. May I help you?"

He watched her blink, the smile about to fade before she got it back.

"The same to you, with sugar on it, dick-face." She hung up and winked at Lyons. "That makes seven threats today. We're on a roll."

A tall man in a polyester suit appeared beside her, frowning at the telephone. "Some kind of problem, Gayle?"

"Another call from Fuck-you Freddie. He's a little late today."

"The trace?"

"I didn't check. You know he always uses pay phones on the beach."

"Okay." The rent-a-cop turned cautious eyes on Lyons. "Can I help you. Mr....?"

"Lewis," Lyons replied, slipping into character. "Chad Lewis. I'm supposed to have a two o'clock appointment with Ms. Teresina."

"Gayle?"

The secretary checked her book, visibly annoyed at having Mr. Polyester breathing down her neck. "Chad Lewis, two o'clock it is."

"A moment, please."

The tall man disappeared, retreating down a narrow corridor, and Lyons waited several moments for him to return. The guy came back as twins—another suit and spit-shined wingtips, regulation haircut . . .

"This way."

He stepped around the waist-high counter, showing the bogus DEA credentials on demand and trailing number one along the corridor, while number two brought up the rear. Lyons's escorts took a right to drop him off at a smallish office fitted out with desk and filing cabinets, two extra chairs, assorted plaques and commendations mounted on the walls.

Maria Teresina rose and came to greet him, offering her hand, and she was even better looking in the flesh than on TV. Dark hair that fell below her shoulders glistened with highlights as she moved. She had a hundred-candlepower smile and eyes that stripped you bare to look inside. All business, Lyons didn't even want to think about the killer body, obvious despite the relatively straitlaced business suit she wore.

"How are you, Mr. Lewis?"

"Great, and I appreciate your taking time to see me, Ms.—"

"Maria, please."

"Okay. Let's make it Chad."

"Some coffee, Chad?"

"I wouldn't turn it down."

He sat, and she poured them both a cup. The polyester twins withdrew and closed the door behind them.

"You take a lot of flak, I guess."

"It comes and goes," she replied. "The real grief's coming down out there, on kids and parents, wives and husbands. Every day, year-round, we've got ODs and murders, every other kind of drug-related crime you can imagine. But ... you know that, right?"

"I heard a rumor."

"You're out of Washington, I think you said?"

"Short-term. I'm what you'd call a trouble-shooter, here today and gone tomorrow."

"That's a shame."

"Well, maybe not tomorrow."

She laughed, and Lyons thought she was beautiful.

"The thing is," he continued, "as you know, we've got a major problem with the drug flow through Miami. I'm not spilling any secrets here. We've got the OMB complaining every time we spend a dime, and Justice snapping at our heels to get results. Between the two, we do our jobs—most of us, anyway."

"But there's a problem? Something else, I mean?"

"Could be. For now let's say I'm looking for a source outside the shop, and let it go at that."

"I see."

"You might get mixed reviews from Metro-Dade, but I can tell you you've got fans in Washington. A couple of them recommended I should get in touch, pick up some names, whatever you might have to help me out before I waste a lot of time duplicating the effort."

"I'll be glad to help you if I can. Exactly what—"

The shock wave toppled Lyons from his chair and dumped him onto the vinyl floor, a rain of plaster sifting down from overhead. His mind was screaming "Earthquake!" but he recognized the sound of an explosion, picking up a telltale smell of dynamite and smoke.

A bomb.

He saw Maria staring at him from behind her desk. "Stay put a minute," he commanded, lurching to his feet and reaching for the big Colt Python holstered underneath his arm.

Lyons wasn't sure if there would be a backup team, but he was ready if they came. A blast of automatic gunfire took out the back door's lock, and they were in, at least two submachine guns hosing down the corridor. He cocked the blue-steel Magnum, crouched and waited, knowing that his enemies would have to show themselves to verify the kill if nothing else.

The first one through the doorway was a slender Cuban with an Uzi in his hands. He started firing as he crossed the threshold, stitching holes across two walls and shattering Maria's glass-framed commendations like a line of targets in a shooting gallery.

The guy never knew what happened as the Colt .357 roared and Lyons shot him in the face at point-blank range. The headless hitter dropped without a twitch, and number two came in behind him, tall and black, his Ingram MAC-10 raking everything in sight.

Lyons drilled the guy in the chest, the slugs punching him against the nearest filing cabinet. His eyes glazed over as he slithered to his knees, then toppled forward onto his face.

The Able warrior scooped up the Cuban's Uzi and checked its load before he hit the doorway, leading with both his Colt and the Israeli stuttergun. The door stood open on an empty corridor, a body clad in blood-soaked polyester stretched out to his left. He could hear a souped-up engine rumbling in the lot out back—the wheelman, waiting for his shooters to return and give him five to indicate a job well done.

He cleared the exit in a combat crouch in case the driver might be covering, and an expression of shock was all he registered before the young Hispanic put his Firebird in reverse and gave it everything he had. Lyons did the same, both weapons going off together. The windshield frosted over for an instant, then imploded as the driver died. His foot on the accelerator didn't know the difference, and the car shot backward on its own, the curving track aborted by destructive impact with a stout brick wall.

Lyons doubled back to check the others, knowing that the second rent-a-cop was dead or badly wounded even as he made the move. Dead won the toss, a jagged piece of wood from the explosion jutting from his chest. The secretary, Gayle, was still alive and semiconscious, bleeding from a scalp wound and perhaps in places Lyons couldn't see.

Her telephone eluded him until he found the cord and traced it, hauling in the plastic base. The receiver was sheared away and lost. He cursed and ran back toward Maria's office, found her waiting at the door, a dazed expression on her face.

"Call 911," he snapped. "We need an ambulance right now."

"Okay."

The menial assignment seemed to bring her back, and Lyons left her to it, making tracks for the reception area again to try his hand at some emergency first aid.

Five dead, and one that might go either way, depending. Someone else had been assigned to toss the bomb out front, and he—or they—were blocks away by now, untraceable unless some witness on the street had made their vehicle and license plate. Maria Teresina was unharmed, by all appearances, and that was something to be thankful for.

Was it coincidence that the shooters turned up a few short moments after he'd arrived?

Such things happened, Lyons knew from past experience. And yet . . .

He sat with Gayle and waited for the sirens, knowing in his gut that it had only just begun. Coincidence or not, the war in Florida was heating up, and Lyons meant to see it boil.

Not matter who got burned.

8

"A calculated insult, nothing more. Costanza hopes to shame me in the public eye."

Raul Rodriguez drained a shot glass as he finished speaking, turned and slammed it against the marble bar with force enough to leave it cracked.

"You can't be sure of that," Lupe Vargas replied, lighting a cheroot and pluming acrid smoke in the direction of the ceiling fans. "I mean, Costanza. Someone else perhaps?"

"Who else despises me enough to do this thing? Who else would have the nerve?"

The dealer's second-in-command shrugged helplessly. "I don't know, Raul. Inquiries have been made, of course, but no one recognized the man. His picture on surveillance cameras—"

"Means exactly nothing! Did I say Costanza robbed the bank *himself*? Of course he hired a stranger, maybe one of his Israelis, but it was his idea. A little joke at my expense. Eight million dollars thrown away or burned, along with deeds and stock certificates, the rest of it."

He didn't have to specify "the rest," as Vargas knew that it included blackmail information—photos, tapes, and so on—that allowed Rodriguez to manipulate a string of politicians both in Medellín and Bogotá. The safe-deposit box wasn't his only stash of such incriminating evidence, by any means, but it had been the largest and most complete.

If word of its destruction spread in certain quarters, he'd have to try a new approach—brute force perhaps—to re-establish his control.

"The helicopter was a rental," Vargas told him, smoking thoughtfully. "We traced it to the dealership and showed the gunman's photograph, but it was hired by someone else. A smaller man, perhaps a European or American. The rental agent was a peasant. Every foreign accent sounds the same to him."

Rodriguez poured himself another double shot of whiskey, slugged it down and set the glass aside. He was surrounded by incompetents and fools.

"A different man," he said, exasperation audible behind the words. "You thought, perhaps, the goddamn helicopter flew itself? It came to fetch the gunman and it carried him away. That *would* require a pilot, wouldn't you suppose?"

"Yes, I would."

"So. You checked the rental papers? Pilots must display their license to arrange a rental, and a foreigner would almost certainly be forced to show his passport."

"Yes, I was about to say—"

"Then say it, Lupe, and be done."

"He identified himself as Jason Grimes. We have the numbers for his pilot's license and his passport—it's American, but possibly a fake."

"Costanza's Israelis are clever. They employ Americans, South Africans—whoever has the skills they need. You're undoubtedly correct about the passport and the license. I'll be surprised if either of them proves to be legitimate."

"At least we know the gunman's face. If we continue searching Medellín—"

"He could be safe in Panama by now. Or halfway back to the United States, if they're finished with him. Search, by all means, but we must prepare ourselves to act on other fronts, as well."

"I don't see what else we can do."

Such fools.

"We can retaliate against Costanza, damn you! Listen to your instinct, if you have no brain. Costanza is responsible for my humiliation. *He* must suffer now as punishment for this affront."

"But how ... ?"

"You're supposed to be my strong right hand. Must I do everything myself?"

"No, sir. But we can't reach Costanza yet. You know we've tried."

"Keep trying. In the meantime find a way for me to hurt him, make him squirm, as he would do to me."

"He has a bank in Bogotá. We could—"

Rodriguez silenced Vargas with a glare. "No banks. I won't run around behind the bastard, copying his movements like a monkey in the zoo. Find something else."

"Yes, sir."

"And make it soon. Costanza might be laughing now, but I'll change his mood."

"At once." With the decision ratified, he sat there, smoking.

"Well, Lupe?"

"Eh?"

The voice was like glacial ice. "Don't let me keep you."

"No, sir. I'll speak with Sanchez and prepare a list of targets so that you can choose."

"Tonight," Rodriguez ordered. "I would like to give Luis a little gift tomorrow morning. Something he can chew with his breakfast."

The silence after Vargas had departed helped Rodriguez to relax. He knew that anger only placed him at Costanza's mercy, prompting him to actions that were rash and reckless. Still, his honor had to be avenged before another day was out, or he'd be ashamed to face himself, much less the hundreds who depended on him as their commander in chief.

But something Vargas had said was eating at him, making him uneasy in his new tranquillity—the possibility of someone else behind his personal embarrassment.

Another enemy.

But who?

Rodriguez pushed the problem out of mind, dismissing it. He knew Costanza, and the man was enemy enough for anyone to deal with in a killing situation. If, by some peculiar twist of fate, Luis *was* innocent of robbing him, exposing him to ridicule, there would be time enough to find the guilty parties later.

After he had put Costanza in his proper place.

THE NIGHTCLUB WAS a favorite with the cream of Medellín society, financed across the board by capital accrued from the Mercado drug cartel. On any given night a stellar list of politicians, wealthy planters and celebrities assembled to rub shoulders with the very dealers who had scandalized their country for a dozen years or more. It was a place where money talked and differences were laid aside in the pursuit of alcoholic gaiety. Police were known to frequent the establishment—at least those officers who raked in graft enough to meet the cover charge—and they appeared to have no qualms about consorting with their prey.

Nor did the Executioner.

In Bolan's often solitary war against the savages, he'd relied from time to time upon a method of disguise he called "role camouflage." In essence the technique relied upon an enemy to "see" what was expected in a given situation, letting the imagination fill in any gaps between anticipation and reality. In Vietnam he had "concealed" himself in the middle of a wide-open rice paddy, donning black pajamas and a coolie hat while Vietcong patrols filed past, ignoring him despite the obvious discrepancy in Bolan's size and general build. The same technique had served him in his one-man war against the Mafia, with Bolan passing through the hostile lines on more than one occasion posing as a member of the mob's elite extermination team. It wasn't foolproof—nothing was, in life—but the approach had served him well enough that Bolan felt secure in trying it again.

He started with the suit, a flashy number that would cost an easy thousand off the rack. As well, he had Italian leather on his feet, a diamond-studded Rolex on his wrist and rings to match. If his Beretta showed a bit beneath the coat, so much the better. In Colombia real men traveled armed.

The place was jumping when he entered, music from a live band filling up the dance floor with attractive couples dressed to make a splash. Initially surprised to find so many blondes in evidence, he finally decided that the lure of narcodollars must have drawn them from the States, as easy money and excitement had been drawing camp followers throughout recorded history. They gave the club an international appeal that would appeal to someone of Mercado's sensibilities.

The maître d' showed Bolan to a table on the sidelines, its relation to the band and stage commensurate with Bolan's tip. He ordered wine to start and sipped it as he scanned the room for faces he might recognize. Mercado wasn't visible, but it had been to much to hope for on a first approach. The plan would work as well without him, and the Executioner was ready to proceed.

Aside from the Beretta in its armpit sling, he carried six incendiary sticks the size of slim cheroots. Inside his waistband, at the back, two smokers nestled snug on either side of Bolan's spine. The size of standard highway flares, upon ignition they'd generate twin clouds sufficient in their mass to simulate a major conflagration on the premises.

A little fire, a lot of smoke, and Bolan would be halfway home.

He finished off the glass of wine and poured himself another, sipping, while the band worked through its set. A waiter came and went, departing with the warrior's order for a filet mignon he didn't plan to eat. Another moment, and he rose to seek out the men's room, a lighted sign directing him.

The washroom was a showplace, sporting marble, tile and polished chrome. An old mestizo dressed in white was standing by, dispensing towels and grinning when he got a tip.

By chance, they had the rest room to themselves. Bolan palmed a hundred-peso note, warning the old man that he should leave without delay. A glimpse of the Beretta made his point, and as the door swung shut behind the man, the Executioner was already planting the incendiaries.

The built-in time delay gave Bolan sixty seconds to ignition, and he used the time outside, dim lighting an accomplice as he left one of the smokers with a potted palm along the way. Instead of seeking out his table Bolan drifted past the dance floor toward the door marked Private, which had caught his eye the moment he'd stepped inside the club. An office, possibly the counting room—whatever, it was worth a look.

He reached the door as smoke erupted from the potted palm and spread across the dance floor, moving rapidly. A woman screamed, immediately followed by a chorus of excited voices, chairs and tables crashing over as the crowd went wild. The men's room would be burning bright by now, a touch of realism just in case the smoker was discovered prematurely.

A guard was posted at the office door, and he reacted swiftly when it hit the fan, a back step, one hand on the knob, a warning on his lips. A straight-arm shot between the shoulders cut him off and carried him across the desk, arms flailing in an effort to regain his balance as the Executioner stepped in and closed the door.

The manager was seated at his desk, eyes locked on the new arrival. A second gunner was at his side. They saw the gun in Bolan's hand and froze, but number one—the human cannonball—was too angry to think as he pushed through the door, his right hand thrust inside his jacket, groping for his piece.

A parabellum mangler got there first, the shooter melting as a hole opened in his forehead and the light clicked off behind his eyes. One down, and all the fight went out of numbers two and three, the second gunner opening his hands and keeping them in sight.

The manager was cool, considering, and his voice was steady as he asked a question in rapid Spanish that Bolan couldn't understand.

"Try English."

"So. What do you want?"

"I'll settle for the cash on hand."

"A robbery?" The guy appeared confused, incredulous, as if a UFO had touched down in his office and the occupants had ordered ginger ale. "There must be some mistake."

"I know your boss, if that's what's on your mind. Let's see the cash."

"You won't enjoy it long."

"My problem. Yours is running out of time."

At a nod from his boss the bodyguard crossed the room with slow, exaggerated strides, hunched down before a safe and spun the dial. He returned to the desk bearing a heavy metal cash box. The manager withdrew a key from his vest pocket, opened it and turned the box around. A glance revealed that it was filled with stacks of notes in various denominations.

"Fair enough." Bolan primed a slim incendiary stick and dropped it into the cash box, then closed the lid and backed away.

"What are you doing?" the manager asked.

"I'm turning up the heat. Your boss is going out of business, but he doesn't know it yet."

"I don't—"

Before the guy could squeeze his question out, there was a flash of heat and light, the cash box melting down before their eyes. In another minute it would be burning through the desk.

The manager jumped up and lurched away, his sidekick using the distraction as a cover when he made his move. It wasn't all that subtle, and the Executioner was waiting for him, squeezing off another parabellum round that bounced him off the nearest wall, dead before he hit the floor.

"Last chance," he told the manager.

They left together, separating in the crush outside as Bolan pitched the second smoker overhand to keep the well-dressed rabble moving. In the parking lot outside a traffic jam was shaping up, with everybody going for his car at once, the handful of valets forgotten, swept aside. Expecting nothing less, the Executioner had parked a block away outside another club, and he was running clear before the sirens started closing in.

Round two, but he was still in the preliminaries, working slowly toward the main event. With any luck Mercado and Rodriguez would begin comparing notes, and both would point accusing fingers at Costanza as the author of their grief.

Day One was winding down, but it was just a start.

The Executioner had barely scratched the surface in his war against the drug cartels, but he was getting there. The ripples had begun to spread.

9

The homicide detectives used up ninety minutes, going over everything three times before they checked out Carl Lyons with the DEA. He told the story straight to Metro-Dade, without the Stony Man connection, standing on his cover as a wild card out of Washington. They let him place a call before the local Feds arrived, and Brognola was obviously quick enough to put a bug in someone's ear and save the play. The regional director turned up with a sour expression on his face, but he confirmed the story of an independent rundown on security.

For all Ironman knew, he might have thought it was the truth.

Score one for Brognola and Stony Man, but they could kiss off any thought of working quietly from that point on. Lyons's face was on TV, his fat was in the fire and any undercover work would fall on Gadgets and Politician now.

One benefit of working in the open was that he was able to inquire about the three men he'd killed. They all had records, free-lance muscle for the most part, with a handful of convictions covering the scale from auto theft to burglary and voluntary manslaughter. Two of them had been arrested on suspicion in a string of drug-related homicides, but murder charges never seemed to stick. The driver was a coke head who had maimed his wife with acid back in 1981 and served a five spot with an extra eighteen months for trying to escape.

Nice boys.

The city wouldn't miss them, but for Lyons's part, he'd have rather taken one or two alive and grilled the bastards for the name of their employer. Anything to lead him one step farther on.

The way it stood, Maria Teresina had so many enemies it was impossible to nail the shooters down without a squeal. They might have been cartel commandos once removed, or someone she'd stepped on with her drive to turn in pushers from the local neighborhoods. The only thing Lyons knew for sure was that the game had escalated from a war of words to bloodshed in the streets.

What else was new?

When they were finished with the shooting team, he drove Maria over to Jackson Memorial Hospital on Twelfth. Her secretary, Gayle, was in intensive care but rated stable, with a decent shot at complete recovery. She was sedated by the time they got there, and they didn't hang around to watch the monitors record her vital signs. Maria left her card and got a promise from the duty nurse to let her know of any changes in the injured woman's status, either way.

Outside, the day's events seemed to overtake her all at once. She leaned against the car while Lyons got the door and shook her hair back, looking pale despite her dark complexion.

"God, I can't believe this! Five men dead and Gayle..."

"You had to know the dealers wouldn't let you skate forever."

Even as he said it, Lyons wished he could take the words back, make them disappear. He hadn't meant to point a finger at Maria, blaming her for anything. The dealers were responsible and no one else.

"I never thought—"

"Hey, look, I'm sorry." It felt funny, saying words he seldom used. "I didn't mean that what went down was your fault. It's a different game, with so much money on the table. People get upset when you start cutting in on sales."

"I didn't really know the men we hired to work security," she said. "It's strange. I signed their checks and saw them almost every day, but I have no idea if they were married, whether they had children…anything at all about their private lives."

"No reason why you should," Lyons answered. "They were paid to do a job, and this one got away from them. Sometimes things just fall apart."

"You managed to recover well enough."

"It's not the first time someone's tried to dust me off."

"And still you do the job?"

"If I quit, they win."

She forced a smile. "It's the same for me."

Lyons met her gaze and didn't look away. "I know."

ONCE THEY BEGAN to drive, Maria was surprised to find that she was hungry. Lyons took the news in stride, his stomach growling at the distant memory of lunch, and told her it was normal, a survivor hanging on. The worst was over—for the moment, anyway—and it was time to live again.

"I can't go out this way," she said. "I'm filthy, and I must look frightful. All that smoke and crawling on the floor."

"It doesn't show," he told her honestly. "If you want to stop somewhere and freshen up, no problem, but I promise you, you look just fine the way you are."

"All right," she said, relenting, "but I have to find an automatic teller first."

"My treat. Or Uncle Sam's. Just pick the spot."

"You save my life and buy me dinner, too?"

"A package deal," he told her, smiling. "Anyhow, I'm off the clock."

He caught her watching, a peripheral impression of her cautious smile.

"So this would be a date?"

"Don't get me wrong," he replied. "We've still got business to discuss, if you're agreeable."

"I see."

"Of course, it doesn't have to be *all* business. The way I see it, you could stand to loosen up a little after all you've been through today."

"Perhaps."

He had the feeling she was laughing at him, maybe teasing, but she kept it to herself. She named a restaurant on Poinciana, twenty minutes south, and Lyons picked up Highway 95 to shave the time.

The café was a Cuban mom-and-pop that kept its steady customers by word of mouth. The food was excellent, as was the service, and the atmosphere a hairbreadth shy of intimate. Lyons sipped imported beer and watched Maria working on her second rum and Coke, surprised at the desire to let himself unwind.

"What brought you to the States?" he asked when they were finished with their salads, waiting for the main course to arrive.

"You know about my country, all the poverty and violence," she replied. "Eleven hundred dollars is the average yearly income for a working man, and women earn far less except for those who sell themselves. My parents left Colombia when I was twelve years old and settled in Miami."

"And?"

"They're both gone now."

"I'm sorry."

"Why?"

The question took him by surprise. "I know how much it hurts to lose someone you care about."

"My father drove a taxi," she went on, as if he hadn't spoken. "When the riots came in 1980, he was caught in

Overtown. A firebomb burst inside his cab. My mother lived another year, but she was never really there. You understand?"

"I've seen it happen."

"So."

"And now you take the dealers on."

"The two events are unrelated, Mr. Lewis."

"Can we make it Chad?"

"Of course. The men who killed my father were like animals, a mob without direction. He was there, and they were there. He died."

"And you've forgiven them?"

"I *understand* them—something of their rage at least. In Bogotá, when I was ten years old, a friend of mine was shot by the police. An accident, they said. We buried her on her eleventh birthday."

"So you've got no love for the police."

Maria shrugged. "I've dealt with the authorities at different levels, in this country and Colombia. Some do their jobs, some nod their heads and look the other way."

"It takes all kinds," Lyons said, knowing that it sounded lame.

"And you?"

"Excuse me?"

"What kind are you?" Her smile helped take the edge off the question. "What makes you put on a badge?"

"To start, I felt like maybe I could make a difference, help someone, you know? We're talking sixties here—the drugs and riots, this and that. It seemed like everything was upside down, and no one had a grip on how to put it right."

"You were a young idealist?"

"Maybe. I don't know. The streets take care of that, right quick. You don't last long with starry-eyed ideals. Before you know it, saving souls goes out the window and you concentrate on punishment."

"And does it work?"

He shrugged. "Well, one thing for sure, those three today, they won't be pulling any more triggers."

"If you can find the man who sent them, will you kill him, too?"

Lyons made a point of putting on his federal agent face. "I'd rather see him doing time," he lied, "but when you come right down to it, the choice is his."

"A part of me would like to see him dead," Maria told him. "It frightens me."

"I'd say it was a natural reaction, given the circumstances. I get ticked off when people try to kill me, too."

"I've noticed. But I haven't thanked you yet."

"For what?"

"My life."

"I did my job, that's all." Their food arrived, the aromatic spices strong enough to clear Lyons's sinuses before he took a bite. "I think I've got myself in trouble here."

Maria smiled across the table at him, beautiful by candlelight, and said, "We'll have to find you something soothing for dessert."

"THE SECOND ON THE LEFT?"

"It's number seventeen."

"Okay."

Politician glanced both ways along the dingy corridor, a naked bulb at either end providing dim illumination. At his side Schwarz stood at ease. One hand was tucked inside his jacket, wrapped around a gun.

"Here goes."

The lock was cheap and easy. Fifteen seconds, give or take, and they were in. The small apartment smelled of garbage, cigarettes and marijuana smoke.

"Some dump."

"Reminds me of a place I used to rent in junior college," Blancanales said.

"You always had great taste."

The flat on Fourth Street had been occupied until that afternoon by Wes Mathis—also known to the police and street associates as Leroy X, Matula al-Shabazz and Blaze. A Muslim ousted by his peers for dealing drugs, he had a ten-year record of adult arrests for grand theft auto, statutory rape, assault and battery, possession of illegal drugs and weapons. On the side, he was suspected as a principal in six or seven contract murders in the past three years, all drug-related, none of them with evidence enough to stand in court.

It wouldn't matter now. The lanky gunner's show had closed that afternoon when he drew down on Lyons and was blown away.

Case closed—except they still had no idea of who had pulled the strings. The one thing Wes Mathis *wasn't* was a wheel, the kind who put a contract out on others and sat back to watch them die. He'd been mercenary muscle from the time he'd started chalking up arrests, at age fifteen, and there was nothing in his file to indicate he'd graduated to the major league. His two companions rated even farther down the scale, and they were known to work with Mathis frequently.

In short, it had been a contract job with Wes catching, signing on a couple of his friends to help. Three up, three down—and that left one, for their connection with the money man.

It was a long shot, tossing the apartment for a clue, because Mathis didn't seem the type to write things down. The police had tossed the flat already, checking it for drugs and weapons, but the men of Able Team had something else in mind.

A simple clue was all they were after, something to move them one link farther up the chain.

It took an hour, but they found it written on the kitchen wall beside the telephone—"E.R.," and a local number following. Politician didn't bother looking for a pen and pad, committing them to memory instead.

"That's it?" Schwarz asked.

"It's more than what we had."

"Some piece of tail, more than likely."

"We'll know for sure when we check it out."

Schwarz grinned. "You think we ought to straighten up a tad before we leave?"

"Get real."

MARIA TERESINA HAD a flat on southwest Twenty-fourth Street, two blocks east of the Miracle Mile. Lyons had expected something in the nature of a friendly brush-off, and he was taken by surprise when Maria invited him inside.

The place was clean and homey, not exactly feminine—more Art Deco, with abstract paintings on the walls and furniture that ran to vinyl over polished chrome. He liked it, though. It struck him as a fair reflection of the lady's personality: assertive, independent, stubborn in refusing to conform.

"A glass of wine? Some coffee?"

"Coffee's fine."

"It's instant."

"Better yet."

He watched her in the kitchen while she worked, enjoying it, a small domestic scene with no responsibility attached. It made him wonder for an instant what he might have missed along the way, but Lyons pushed the thought aside and concentrated on his job.

"You need some new security," he commented.

"I'll make the call tomorrow."

"What about tonight?"

Maria glanced at him and frowned. "I can't believe they'd try again so soon."

"You might be right, but why take chances?"

Glancing at her watch, she said, "I couldn't call the agency tonight. It's much too late."

"Some free advice? Call up a friend you trust and spend the night, or have her come and stay with you."

She poured the coffee, bringing cups for both of them, and sat beside him on the couch. "With Gayle..." Maria shook her head. "I really couldn't ask."

He took the plunge. "Suppose somebody volunteered?"

He gaze was cool, direct enough to make him squirm. "Such as?"

"Well, let me think." He made a face, feigned concentration, finally snapped his fingers as it came to him. "I've got it."

"Oh?"

"I'm all alone in town, a stranger, and I'm here already. If you've got an extra pillow, I could camp out on the couch, no sweat."

Maria shook her head again. "I'm sorry. That won't do at all."

"Well, I just thought—"

"The couch, I mean."

He blinked. "Say what?"

"It's old and too uncomfortable. I insist you come to bed."

Before he had a chance to speak, Maria leaned in and kissed him on the mouth, her own lips parting to admit his tongue. Lyons felt himself respond at once, his left hand gliding up to find her breast. Maria offered no resistance as he stroked her, drew her close and pulled her down on top of him.

So far the couch felt fine.

Her hunger seemed to match his own, their hands exploring, pushing clothes aside and fumbling buttons open as they bared strategic skin without undressing. Lyons slipped both hands inside her open blouse and found the catch that held her bra in place, releasing it and easing lacy cups aside to free her breasts, the nipples taut and warm against his lips. Maria's skirt had ridden up around her hips, and Lyons curled his fingers under the elastic waistband of her panties, tugging at them urgently until she freed one hand to help. The secret fold of flesh between her legs was hot and moist.

She sat up, gasping, with his hand trapped underneath her, fumbling at his belt and fly. It took a moment, but she got it, and he raised his hips to help her, tensing as she wriggled back and bent to play him like a clarinet. Lyons tangled fingers in her hair to guide her, but she knew exactly what to do. She brought him to the brink, then pulled away and mounted him, the merger of their flesh like liquid fire.

For something like a heartbeat, Lyons caught himself and realized that he'd lost his objectivity, but what the hell? It didn't happen every day, and if it jeopardized his job performance he'd know it, wouldn't he.

Damn straight.

She rode him to the finish in another moment, thrusting with her hips and taking him along, no matter how he tried to play it out. His need and her determination came together, merged and brought it off before Lyons had a chance to catch himself. One instant, he was holding on and praying it could last; the next, he felt himself disintegrating, fractured atoms hurtling across the cosmos at the speed of light.

They lay together afterward, Maria still on top and holding him inside. He scarcely felt her weight at all.

"You're wrong about the couch," he said when he could breathe again. "It feels all right to me."

"I promise you'll prefer the bed."

"Well, if you think so..."

"Shall I prove it?"

Lyons found the strength to smile. "I'm in your hands."

10

The telephone connection was imperfect, but José Mercado had no trouble understanding every word the caller said. His fingers clutched the receiver tight enough to make his knuckles blanch, his perspiration making him imagine that the plastic had begun to melt.

"I understand."

His voice was firm, completely in control. Mercado was amazed sometimes by the inherent power locked within himself. Another man in his position might have picked up the offending telephone and hurled it through the nearest window.

Power was the key to everything.

"I'll be on the next flight back to Medellín," he told Rodriguez, concentrating on the tenor of his voice.

"Is that advisable?"

"We have no choice," Mercado replied. "Costanza shits on both of us and rubs our noses in it. He must pay."

"I can take care of it myself."

"I want to see his face and watch him die."

"We have no proof he was responsible," the distant voice reminded him.

"You know our enemy as well as I. We aren't lawyers, after all."

"The gunman was American," Rodriguez said. "I'm convinced the same man robbed my bank and caused the damage to your nightclub."

"A mercenary, then. I've already taken steps against Costanza's contact in Miami. It's time we moved against the man himself."

"Agreed. I have a place where you can stay in case F-2 or DAS are still on guard around your house."

Mercado scowled at the mention of his other enemies. F-2 was the official designation for Colombian police intelligence. The DAS—Department of Administrative Security—was roughly equivalent to the American FBI, an arm of government involved in tracking extradition cases since the major drug cartels declared their open season on opposing judges, politicians and attorneys.

"Where else would they be?" Mercado asked sarcastically. "It's not as if they have a decent job of work to do."

Rodriguez laughed appreciatively. "Call me back when you've arranged a flight. I'll meet your plane."

"Of course."

Mercado knew his friend was less concerned with the amenities than mutual security. If the Costanza syndicate was primed for all-out war, with the police and military standing by to strike at any time, they'd be facing enemies on every side. The usual precautions simply weren't good enough.

Mercado booked the flight himself, avoiding middlemen who might have leaked his ETA to hostile ears. He used an alias selected from the telephone directory, avoiding pseudonyms he'd used on previous occasions. A breach in his security would mean direct betrayal by Rodriguez, and he had no fears on that account.

They needed each other in order to survive.

In time, when they'd managed to eliminate Costanza and absorb his operation, buying off or killing off their enemies in government, there would be ample opportunity for him to reassess Rodriguez on the basis of performance under fire. Thus far Raul had been his strong right arm—no mental giant, but a streetwise operator who had courage when it counted. He'd killed eleven men himself—eleven that Mercado knew about—and he'd been for taking on Costanza earlier before Mercado thought the time was right.

Tonight all doubt had been eradicated from his mind.

Costanza must have gone insane to flaunt himself this way. The move against Rodriguez, taking down his private bank, incinerating cash, scattering some in the street, had been a madman's gambit, pushing toward a state of total war. When he attacked Mercado's favorite nightclub, he ensured that the two men would stand together in the fight, their troops united in a drive to crush Costanza.

It was a fact that he retained numerical advantages, in spite of everything. He had more men and guns, more liquid cash on hand, more contacts moving his cocaine in the United States. But he was still one man, no more invincible than any other when the guns went off. A single well-aimed shot would do the trick, if they could only track him down.

And that, of course, would be the problem.

Costanza had been "hiding out" in Medellín for the past two years, since various indictments had been handed down in the United States. It was a fact that he spent several days a week on his estate due north of Medellín, but the authorities could never catch him there, primarily because of bribes Costanza paid to guarantee a warning in advance of any raid.

It would be too much to expect for the police to run him down and lock him in a cage where he would be an easy target prior to extradition. No, Mercado knew he'd have to do the work himself, and in a strange way he was glad.

It was a game, of sorts, like hunting in the forest near his village when he was a boy. The animals could run and hide, but in the end he always found them out and cut them down.

This time Costanza was his quarry in a hunt with everything at stake.

José Mercado knew he wouldn't have had it any other way.

THE SCHOOL OUTSIDE Medellín professed an interest in security, and that was accurate . . . up to a point. It was correct to say that students learned the ins and outs of firearms, martial arts, evading hot pursuit, but they weren't executive chauffeurs or bodyguards, the usual students of training courses on security procedures and techniques. Instead, they were selected from the major street gangs found in Cali, Bogotá and Medellín—and from the drug cartels themselves.

It was a murder school, in plain and simple terms, devoted to ensuring that the criminal elite were never short of skillful hands to do their dirty work. While courses covered unarmed combat, marksmanship and various procedures for "disarming" bombs, the campus specialty was the education of *sicarios*, the motorcycle-riding young gunmen whose attacks had been a trademark of the drug cartels during the past ten years.

Mack Bolan knew the school was organized by Isaac Auerbach and his associate, Chaim Feldman; it was also known that neither man had been observed on campus—or in Medellín—in the past four months. Their staff was capable enough, and life went on without the founders of the school, preparing each new graduating class for its participation in La Violencia.

If anybody asked—which various policemen and attorneys did from time to time—the school was theoretically involved in training personnel to guard executives against attack. They *did* give courses on defusing several kinds of bombs, with the explosive charges detonated now and then employed as demonstrations of the risk involved in failure. Classes *were* conducted in evasive driving, and it was a mere coincidence if certain graduates preferred to use their newfound skills evading the police. Of course, two-wheeled attacks on limousines and other vehicles were simulated at the school—how else could an executive chauffeur learn to defend his clients and himself?

All systems go, on paper, and the government had found no legal grounds for shutting down the school thus far. At times like these it was a point of satisfaction for the Executioner that he wasn't constrained by rules of evidence, the burdens of conclusive proof in court.

He knew what they were up to at the school, damn right.

And school was out as of today.

Grimaldi drove the rented limousine. It was a comedown from his usual mode of airborne transportation, but it fit their needs. The chauffeur's uniform was cut with extra room to hide the service-issue automatic in its armpit holster, and Jack had ready access to a mini-Uzi tucked beneath the driver's seat. The limo wasn't armored, but its souped-up mill would clock 110 at need.

Mack Bolan rode in back, decked out in expensive threads and gold-rimmed aviator's glasses. With any luck the cover would be adequate to get him in, and after that the plan would have to take care of itself.

Finesse would only carry him so far.

In front of Bolan, to his right and hidden on the floorboard, lay a carbon copy of Grimaldi's submachine gun, extra magazines and frag grenades, all covered by a lap rug, safe from prying eyes. It was impractical to plan their moves with any real precision once they passed the compound gates, but they'd taken every step that he could think of to reduce the odds.

The limo's trunk was packed with bargain-basement luggage, each bag filled with dirt to give them traction and prevent—the warrior hoped—a lucky shot from drilling through to score on human flesh.

They both wore Kevlar vests beneath their clothes, for what it might be worth. Damn little in the case of head shots or a tag below the belt.

Grimaldi had rehearsed evasive measures with the limo, using up a tank of gas and sixty minutes' worth of precious time before he satisfied himself that he could make the bulky rig perform on cue.

As for the Executioner, he was committed to succeed or die.

And it could still go either way.

"We're there," Grimaldi announced, and the Executioner saw the gates in front of them. An eight-foot chain-link fence with razor wire on top stretched out at least a hundred yards in each direction. Buildings stood on the left, and something like an oval racetrack was located in the center of the compound. To their right was a mock-up city street, reminding him of something you'd see during the tour at Universal Studios.

As they pulled up outside the gates, the sound of racing motorcycle engines reached them through the tinted windows of the limousine. Two midsize bikes appeared at one end of the track, the drivers running neck and neck along the straightaway and leaning toward the nearest curve. As far as Bolan could tell, neither one was armed.

The gate man wore a uniform with a Sam Browne belt that held a pistol on his right hip and a walkie-talkie on the left. His age was indeterminate, somewhere between the mid-twenties and a well-kept thirty-five. Bolan could feel that his stocky build was all muscle. The man's suspicious eyes flicked back and forth between Grimaldi and the Executioner, his right hand covering the Llama automatic on his hip.

Grimaldi hit a button and the driver's window powered down. The gate man tried his Spanish on for size, then switched to English when Grimaldi shrugged and rolled his eyes.

"You have an appointment?"

"That's why we're here," Grimaldi replied. "To make one. If you want folks to call ahead, you ought to put your number in the book."

"Instructors are busy now."

"Who isn't? Look, we don't expect a class today, you follow? Maybe we could have a word or two with the director, set up a schedule."

"I'll have to ask."

"Why don't you do that?"

The gate man stepped away, still watching them as he freed the walkie-talkie from its harness, lifted it and spoke. The answer was inaudible to Bolan, but he watched the gate man nod, as if his contact on the other end could see. Another moment, and he stepped back toward the car.

"Your names?"

"I'm just the driver, pal." Grimaldi wore a plastic smile and cocked a thumb across his shoulder. "This here is Mr. Michael Ballentine of the Miami Ballantines. They're big in pharmaceuticals up there, you get my drift? He heard about your little setup here, and we drove out to talk about security arrangements for his business interests in Colombia. I mean, that *is* your line?"

"Of course."

The man stepped back hastily and muttered into the radio, while Bolan held his breath and waited for the dice to hit their mark. It was unlikely anyone inside the compound had connections in Miami, and the name of Ballentine would draw a blank, in any case.

The gate man put his radio away and fumbled through a limp salute before he turned back to the guardhouse, stepping in to flip a switch that rolled the gate away on hidden tracks.

"Not bad," Grimaldi said.

"It will be," Bolan promised him, and reached down for the lap rug on the floor.

Grimaldi didn't care much for the plan, but it was all they had. He would have liked a Cobra gunship or a fighter plane to blow the frigging school away, but he had to play it Striker's way.

Once inside, he watched the rearview mirror. The gate rolled shut behind them, and the guard on station tracked them across the thirty yards of open ground that lay between their point of entry and the main administration building, which was set back twenty feet inside the chain-link fence. Grimaldi parked and left the engine running as he stepped back, opening the door for Bolan.

He watched the Executioner climb the steps of the administration building, a suit out front meeting him with a handshake and a smile before they disappeared inside. Grimaldi turned to face the track, where there were now three street bikes circling, a new four-door sedan behind them, keeping pace.

Grimaldi watched the bikers park along the verge with engines idling, one consulting briefly with the other two—their teacher?—while the dark sedan rolled on. They let it pass them twice, but on the second time around two bikes fell in behind. They paced the target for a lap before they made their move, pulling their weapons out from under denim jackets—one of them an Ingram, the other an unmistakable 7.65 mm Skorpion. The hardware didn't show when they were driving—from a distance, anyway—but it would do the job, and no mistake.

They made their strafing run like members of a crack precision drill team, splitting up to flank the car and pouring on the gas when their intended mark began to make his escape run. It was tricky, but they had the move down cold—a surge of hidden power to pass the car on either side before they swiveled in their seats to catch the driver in a cross fire, peppering the doors and windshield of the target vehicle with bullets made of colored wax.

Economy, and still it registered the hits. From what Grimaldi saw, the two-wheeled team had scored a relatively easy kill.

And then all hell broke loose.

The second round of shots was muffled, covered by the intervening walls, but Grimaldi could hear them all the same. He reached beneath the driver's seat and pulled out the mini-Uzi as Bolan cleared the steps of the administration building. The warrior paused long enough to lob a frag grenade before he turned and sprinted for the car. Behind him the explosion shattered windows, and a jagged section of the building's metal roof swung back as if it were a trapdoor on a hinge.

"Let's roll!" the big man snapped as he slid in behind Grimaldi and his door clicked shut.

"I hear you."

The dark sedan had coasted to a stop, its driver staring through a window marked with wax. Grimaldi saw the bikers in a huddle, one guy pointing as if the others weren't quite smart enough to figure out that they had a problem on their hands. Downrange, around a kind of cinder-block garage, another six or seven men were milling in the open bays and nudging one another, falling back to reach their vehicles and guns.

"You up for cutting class?" Grimaldi asked.

"Seems like the thing to do."

"Hang on." He put the mini-Uzi in his lap and gripped the steering wheel. "The truant policy around this place is murder."

They reached the simulated street scene before the other bikers caught them, six new sets of wheels with two men riding double on a Honda at the tag end of the pack. They all had guns in view, the only unknown quantity their chase car, daubed with colored wax like droppings from a flock of dysenteric gulls. Would the intended target of the killer exercise be armed? And would it matter if he rammed the limousine and stalled them out?

Once on the set, it was apparent they'd underestimated the facilities. Instead of one street flanked by the facades of buildings, carpenters had laid out intersections, alleyways, a simulated "town" perhaps three blocks in length and two across. Grimaldi took the left-hand turn and cut it short, his fender slamming one of the pursuit bikes, while another tried to veer away from its collision course and slammed head-on into a plywood wall.

They made the turn on screaming tires and ran for half a simulated block with four remaining cycles on their tail before Grimaldi yelled, "Hang on!" He hit the brakes as Bolan braced himself, three bikers swerving past without an opportunity to aim and fire, the fourth machine unmanageable, skidding broadside into a collision with the limo's bullet-riddled trunk. The driver screamed, his right leg crushed between the bike and car, and Bolan silenced him with a precision burst across the deck.

Another heartbeat, and Grimaldi had the vehicle back in motion, the pursuer now, with three bikes up ahead and no sign of the dark sedan behind. The cyclists knew their drill, all right, two of them making for the nearest cross street, but the third was slower, weighed down with an extra rider on the back. Grimaldi overtook the Honda with a burst of speed and swung his wheel to make connection with a jarring crash, the cycle and its rider airborne, while the passenger was sucked beneath the limo and reduced to mangled flesh on broken bones.

Grimaldi floored it and followed the escaping cycles right around the block, a box that met the dark sedan approaching from the west. It was a lethal game of chicken played at twenty yards with motorcycles in between, one biker dropping his Suzuki in an effort to avoid the trap, his comrade hanging on and hoping for a miracle.

The Stony Man flyboy held the limo steady to the final instant, veering slightly to the right as his opponent swung a foot the other way to pass them on the driver's side. It would have been enough without the motorcycle in between, but as it was they made a sandwich of the man and his machine, his death cry swallowed by the sound of rending metal.

As the dark sedan scraped by, Bolan fired his Uzi through the open window, tracking on the driver's silhouette from point-blank range. The four-door carried no more armor than their limousine, and the warrior watched the wheelman's skull dissolve beneath a spray of parabellum rounds. He used another burst to tag the biker who had dropped his cycle in the street. Then Grimaldi said, "We're out of here," reversing toward the center of the compound with a rattle starting underneath the hood.

The gate man saw them coming, all alone and reaching for his side arm, but he reconsidered, breaking for the nearest cover as they made a beeline for the gate. They let him go, the car's momentum punching through the chain-link fence.

"This thing could use an overhaul," Grimaldi remarked, grinning into the rearview mirror.

"Will it take us where we need to go?"

"No sweat. I'm glad I didn't sign for the insurance coverage, though."

11

Yakov Katzenelenbogen stood across the street for nearly half an hour prior to entering the supper club. Surveillance was a cheap insurance policy, and while he had a tendency to trust his source at the Israeli embassy, he also knew that drugs and the attendant cash surrounding them had clouded more exalted minds, corrupted more important officers before tonight.

Indeed, if it weren't for the corruption spawned by drugs, the men of Phoenix Force would never have been sent to Panama. Eradicating dealers would be relatively simple, once the vermin were deprived of their political protection, crooked cops and high-priced lawyers, judges bribed or frightened into throwing cases out of court.

Somebody said that money made the world go round, and that was true in crime as much—or more so—than in any other field of human enterprise. While legislators, law-enforcement officers and chief executives were subject to the bribes and blackmail tactics of the *narcotraficantes,* justice would continue limping when it should have run full speed ahead.

This time at least the tip was good.

At nineteen minutes, creeping up on twenty, Isaac Auerbach arrived by chauffeured limousine, alone, and told a joke that made the doorman smile before he disappeared inside. Katz would have known him anywhere—the eye patch, graying hair, the trim physique that showed he hadn't lost his taste for working out each day. The suit looked custom-tailored, and the limousine suggested Auerbach had been successful in his chosen field.

Preparing mercenaries for their several wars—all right. Katz wouldn't fault him there. It was the rest of it—the training of assassins for the drug cartels without regard to the morality of his involvement—there the one-armed veteran of Mossad was forced to draw the line.

They weren't so different really when he stopped to think about it. Both had followed common routes to reach their present situations in the world, defending Israel from her enemies in combat and in cloak-and-dagger roles. Each had been wounded in the cause—an arm, an eye—but fighting on in spite of what their nominal superiors initially described as disabilities, retiring into "private life" as opportunities arose to strike another blow against their enemies.

Except that Auerbach had somehow lost direction, turned himself around, his good eye losing sight of right and wrong. Today he sold his martial skills to those who undermined society with drugs, corruption, random bloodshed in the streets. If not a terrorist himself, he had at least become their tutor, selling out and soiling every memory that Katz cherished of their time together in Mossad.

They had been friends, as such things go, without tremendous overlapping in their private lives. They socialized from time to time, of course, but it was on the job that Katz and Auerbach had measured each other for the most part, striving toward the common goal of Israel's preservation and security. It had been Katz who had left the service first, but now he understood that Auerbach hadn't been far behind, embittered by his treatment at official hands, thinskinned beyond all logic for a man in his profession.

Was he getting even with the world, as well as getting rich by training murderers for the Colombian cartels?

The only way Katz knew of to discover that was to walk up and ask the man.

He had a reservation, and his stylish suit passed muster with the doorman, even if the young valets were startled by his lack of wheels. Katz had a car nearby, but he wasn't about to put the keys in someone else's hands, especially when a hasty exit might be all that saved his life.

Inside, he met the maître d' and told him he was dining with Señor Auerbach. It did the trick, and he was guided to a semiprivate dining room in back, sequestered from the crowd out front. The layout featured candles on the tables, muted lighting fixtures recessed into ceiling tiles, expensive carpeting beneath his feet.

"*Señor,* your guest."

The mercenary caught himself before his mouth dropped open, and he flashed a smile, recovering with fine aplomb. "How long?" he asked, apparently referring to the years since they had seen each other in the flesh.

"A bit."

"And now I see you here."

"So it would seem."

"Coincidence perhaps?"

"There's no such thing," Katz replied, quoting from an aphorism of their service days.

"So be it. You're well?"

Katz shrugged and frowned. "I'd rather hear what you've been doing with yourself."

"What makes me think your question is superfluous, I wonder?"

"Intuition?"

"Possibly. You know about my difference of opinion with Mossad?"

"The bare essentials. I'd be interested in hearing your account."

"There isn't much to say. Despite their public posturing, our leaders have become old women. Press releases and elections mean more to them now than safety for our people. I refused to coddle Arab terrorists, and so we reached a parting of the ways."

"And now?"

"I'm self-employed, as you must surely know."

"A teacher."

"Counterterrorism and security techniques. A real growth industry these days."

"Your clients are Israelis?"

"Yakov, please. Must you insult us both by this charade?"

"All right, then, Isaac. Why the drugs? What are you thinking of?"

"Myself for once. Who has a better right? I literally gave my life for Israel—never mind the eye—and now I'm shunned by sniveling politicians who have never done the dirty work themselves. Survival is the issue, Yakov, as it always was."

"With all the wars and conflict in the world, you choose a country where the drug lords are devouring society, and then you side with them. Is that your definition of survival?"

"I'm not responsible for the narcotics problem. The Americans want drugs and pay outlandish prices for their pleasure. *I* don't supply the chemicals. I'm a soldier, sharing knowledge and experience with others who might have to fight one day."

"Assassins."

Auerbach's eyes turned cold. A waiter was approaching, but he waved the man away. "I've heard that term before," he snapped. "A learned statesman once applied it to myself."

"We aren't discussing politics. The animals you train are nothing more than terrorists themselves. You read the papers, Isaac. You know what's been happening in Bogotá and Medellín, in the United States and Europe. Trigger-men *you* trained denigrating everything you stand for.''

"Make it past tense, Yakov. I no longer stand for any-thing except myself. My country has disowned me, branded me a murderer. I seek companionship among my own.''

"Self-pity doesn't suit you, Isaac.''

"How about self-interest, then? In all the time I was working for Mossad, I scarcely had a bank account. No wife or children, most of my expenses paid when I was on a job—it hardly mattered. When you're cut adrift without resources, you begin to think in terms of caring for your-self. In the United States I think they call it looking out for number one.''

"And what about honor?''

"It's fine for those who can afford it. As it happens, I sleep very well at night—on satin sheets, in fact, and sel-dom by myself. I've discovered that the mercenary life has its rewards.''

"I always thought an honest mercenary fought for cause, as well as cash.''

"You were deceived as I was,'' Auerbach replied. "There are no 'honest' mercenaries, only men who managed to delude themselves that they are saviors of mankind.''

"You obviously cherish no such fantasy.''

"Why should I? What has mankind ever done for me? Some trinkets handed out when I was wounded in the line of duty, promises of a pathetic pension when I grew too old to fight.''

"You wanted public adoration, Isaac?''

"No! Respect would have sufficed. I spent the best part of my life in service to the state, and I was shit on for my trouble. Even so I've rejected offers from the Arab states and others who wish harm on Israel. I do business half a world away, and still they send you after me like an aveng-ing angel.''

Katz eyed his former friend. "You think I was sent from Tel Aviv?"

"Where else?" Slow recognition dawned on Auerbach. "Of course, I should have known. You work for the Americans these days. And you call me a mercenary!"

"I've never killed for money, Isaac. Can you say the same?"

"But you're paid, I daresay. Or is this an act of charity?"

Katz saw that he was getting nowhere. He could kill this man at once, extend his artificial hand and fire the .22 at point-blank range, but he might well create more problems than he solved. "I thought I knew you once," he said.

"You were mistaken, I suspect." The waiter tried again, and this time Auerbach allowed him to approach the table. "I shall dine alone, I think."

Katz nodded, rising from his chair. "I've lost my appetite."

"A clear-cut case of hyperactive scruples. You could use a rest."

"Not yet. I still have work to do."

"Be careful, Yakov."

"Always."

As Katz left, he felt Auerbach watching him until he cleared the private dining area. The maître d' appeared confused but made no move to intercept him, and the doorman stood aside to let him pass.

Outside, the air felt clean and fresh, despite the temperature and city smells. With Auerbach, Katz felt as if he had inhaled the cloying fumes of decadence, a rank miasma of the soul.

He had no doubt that Auerbach would have to be eliminated in order to complete their job in Panama, but it wasn't the proper time or place.

THE CALL from Pablo Arevalo reached McCarter in his hotel room at half past noon, and they arranged the meet for eight o'clock that night. The captain had a place in mind—a relatively cheap downtown hotel—and there appeared to be no point in arguing. McCarter could show up as early as he liked to scout the place, retreating if he smelled a trap. As for a guarantee of absolute security...

There was no such animal, McCarter thought, as he approached the meeting place on foot. His rental car was parked a block away outside a tavern where the clientele was mostly upper middle class. He wasn't concerned about it being stolen in the relatively short time he planned to be away.

A simple in-and-out, collect the "proof" that Arevalo had collected of a link between Caseros and the drug cartels and take it back for group assessment by the team before they passed it on to Brognola. If it was hot enough, the Justice crowd would place it in the hands of sympathetic congressmen at a strategic moment, ammunition to defeat the critics if and when Caseros had to go.

He circled the hotel, examining the nearby shops and windows of apartments on the floors above each storefront and scanning cars and pedestrians along the way. It was entirely possible that he had missed a crack surveillance team, McCarter knew, but there was nothing obvious to indicate he was being watched or lured into a trap.

And what about the captain? Was he really as secure as he appeared? McCarter didn't know where the man had phoned from to arrange the meet or who might have been listening. If Arevalo was a target of surveillance, then the enemy knew how to track him down at any given moment. The thought wasn't a reassuring one, but there was nothing he could do about it now.

The desk clerk didn't seem to see McCarter as he entered the lobby, moved toward the elevator, then veered off on second thought to take the stairs. One means of access was as easy to secure as the other, but at least the stairs would give him room to maneuver if there was trouble. In case of ambush in an elevator, there was little he could do but stand his ground and die.

The third floor seemed deserted, and he moved along the corridor with easy strides, his jacket open, granting easy access to the automatic slung beneath his arm. Eight doors stretched in front of him, odd numbers on the left and even on the right. He bypassed room 21 and doubled back to execute the coded knock, standing aside in case gunfire was blasted through the door.

The captain still hadn't put on his uniform. Tonight he wore a leisure suit, no tie, his shirt unbuttoned at the throat. His smile seemed genuine, but there was caution in his eyes as he leaned out and glanced both ways along the empty corridor. "Come in."

"I thought you'd never ask."

"You weren't followed?"

"Not that I could tell. Yourself?"

The captain shook his head and cocked a thumb in the direction of a low-slung coffee table where a slim manila envelope had been deposited. "Your evidence."

McCarter sat, opened the envelope and extracted several glossy black-and-whites—six shots in all, which were enlarged to eight-by-tens.

The first depicted General Caseros in his full-dress uniform accompanied by three men dressed in flashy business suits. Two of the men were strangers to McCarter, but he recognized the third as Esteban Ortega, rated number two in the Costanza drug cartel. Ortega's sidekicks would be bodyguards, accountants—any way you sliced it, they were clearly on the dealer's team.

The second shot was similar—same group, same day, unless they never changed their clothes. In this one both the general and Ortega stood in profile to the camera, facing each other. They were shaking hands and smiling, as thick as thieves. Which was precisely what they were.

In number three the scene had changed. A night shot, taken from a vehicle outside a private home, the address clearly visible. McCarter reckoned he could track it down, if necessary, and determine ownership if anybody cared. Caseros stood outside the house in casual dress, half hidden by the shadows but identifiable. His lone companion was a smudge, unrecognizable, but he'd shifted by the time the cameraman snapped photo number four.

McCarter smiled as he identified José Mercado, chief among Costanza's competition, lately number one on the Costanza hit parade. "Not bad. Your general plays both ends against the middle, eh?"

"He takes from everyone without distinction, the bastard."

Finishing the stack, McCarter frowned at two shots of a smallish room with cryptic symbols painted on the walls, a table standing in the middle foreground. On the table, jumbled in with objects he couldn't recognize, McCarter saw a chalice, several knives, a wooden bowl and what appeared to be a chicken—gutted, with its head removed. "What's this?"

"The witch room," Arevalo answered with a scowl. "Your government already knows about the drugs, but do they know Caseros is insane? He offers sacrifices to the gods of Santeria, seeking their protection. Goats, chickens and lambs—some say he has even sacrificed a child."

"No snaps connecting him with this?"

"It wasn't possible. The ceremonies are a private thing, you understand. One of his bodyguards secured these photographs when he was out of town. The room you see is in the basement of the presidential palace."

"Lovely."

Even as he spoke, McCarter knew the last two shots were wasted, lacking any concrete link between Caseros and the strange religious articles, but he'd send them off in any case. It never hurt to know your target's quirks, his strengths and weaknesses, before you were committed to move against him.

McCarter slipped the photos back inside the envelope and closed the flap. He was about to rise when he saw Arevalo stiffen and turn toward the door. A scuffling sound of footsteps emanated from the hallway, growing louder as a group of six or seven men approached room 21 with no attempt at stealth.

"A trap!" the captain snarled, reaching underneath his jacket for a pistol and spinning toward McCarter in a rage, convinced he'd been betrayed.

He never had a chance to use it as a burst of automatic gunfire ripped through the door and caught him in the side, the impacts spinning him around and dumping him across the nearby bed. McCarter leaped across the coffee table, breaking for the window, his gun in hand before he got there, ready to defend himself.

The enemy was there ahead of him. A shadow stood on the fire escape outside, the muzzle of a weapon smashing through the pane of glass. McCarter triggered two quick rounds and watched the shadow topple backward, vanishing beyond the metal rail, then he had to duck as more rounds ripped through the door, its lock exploding, plaster raining from the walls and ceiling.

He had time to flick the window latch and raise the lower sash before the door gave way behind him, bodies jostling in the open space. They came in firing aimlessly, a sweep around the room, and he was ready with a double punch to knock the point man off his feet before he cleared the windowsill and gave himself to gravity.

Bullets whistled around McCarter's ears. He wrapped both arms around his head, still clutching at the gun and envelope, and lunched himself downstairs. It was a jolting ride that left him bruised and aching, but it saved his life.

The landing on the second floor was low enough for him to risk the drop, and he was into free-fall by the time the first of his assailants reached the window, leaning out and firing blindly into darkness.

Run!

The narrow alleyway was lined with garbage cans and littered with a carpet of debris. McCarter ran, dodging wild rounds from the fire escape and thankful that lights had never been installed to make the alley safer for pedestrians.

When he was almost to the street, a car turned in ahead of him, its headlights blazing bright enough to blind him. He heard the doors open and sensed the weapons leveled at him from a range of fifteen feet. Behind him runners in the darkness cut off his retreat.

The choice was his. One shot, and they would surely cut him down without a second thought. There was no guarantee that they would spare his life, in any case, but if they weren't firing yet . . .

McCarter made his mind up, raised his hands without relinquishing the pistol or manila envelope. He was prepared to die if necessary, but he didn't feel inclined toward suicide.

"Your move," he told the men surrounding him, regretting it as one of them stepped up behind him and put all his weight behind a punch that drove McCarter to his knees.

To hell with it.

He swiveled, bringing up the pistol, but he made the move too late. A gun butt slammed against his skull and fireworks detonated in his head, the bright sparks fading instantly to black.

12

The flight from Panama was right on time, and Raul Rodriguez had his limo waiting at the airstrip, flanked by smaller, faster cars that boasted complements of four men each, all armed with automatic weapons. Two more gunners waited in the limousine, allowing him some privacy in back, and he was confident he could deal with any opposition they encountered on the road.

His men were spaced around the airfield, covering the tree line, when the small plane circled into its approach and touched down on the single landing strip, the pilot feathering his engines as he taxied to a halt beside the waiting cars.

A pair of gunmen were the first outside, José Mercado following when he received the signal that it was safe. Two more bodyguards filed out behind him, bulges conspicuous underneath their coats.

Mercado didn't smile as he approached Rodriguez, but they did shake hands, embracing afterward in the established Latin style. At a hand sign from Rodriguez his troops began their trek back to the cars, relieved that they hadn't been called upon to face an enemy in darkness.

"You had a peaceful flight?" Rodriguez asked.

"It gave me time to think." Mercado's tone was solemn, like a man preparing to deliver some unwelcome bit of news. "My men?"

"Of course."

Curtly issued instructions set off a game of musical chairs. Three of Mercado's men would wedge themselves into the chase cars, while the fourth swapped places with the shotgun rider in the limousine. It was a mere formality, but Raul Rodriguez knew he couldn't expect Mercado to embark upon a journey while his bodyguards were left behind.

Not even riding with his friends.

It was a hazard of the cocaine trade, Rodriguez understood. The only friends a man could really trust were those who died along the way. Survivors, by the very fact of their existence, knew the tricks and tactics of deceit that moved *la merca* from the jungle camps to the refineries, and on from there to waiting customers in the United States. A man who lasted in the trade, by definition, was a ruthless opportunist—probably a murderer and certainly a cheat.

If life was cheap in smugglers' paradise, it could be said that trust was less than worthless. Worse: if you allowed yourself to trust, it would inevitably get you locked away or killed.

Rodriguez didn't trust Mercado—didn't even like him, if it came to that—but circumstance had joined them in a common cause. Together they were nearly strong enough to challenge the Costanza syndicate for ultimate control. They had discussed the possibilities a thousand times, devising theoretic strategies, and now it seemed they'd have no choice but to proceed.

Costanza had thrown down the gauntlet, shaming both of them in public, and he had to die. It was a simple case of quid pro quo. They must destroy their enemy or die in the attempt.

And afterward, if they survived, what then?

It was a subject both men had considered privately, but it had never been discussed. Elimination of Costanza meant the pie would be divided equally instead of cut three ways . . . or would it?

In his heart Rodriguez knew Mercado wanted every gram of coke and every peso for himself. He recognized this basic fact because he felt the same. One-half was better than one-third, but why should a successful trader have to share the wealth at all?

If they destroyed Costanza, there would come a time, inevitably, when Rodriguez and Mercado had to face each other for the final test. Today, however, they were allies of a sort, united in their opposition to the common enemy.

"Your office?" Rodriguez asked.

"Not tonight, I think."

Rodriguez nodded understanding. "Then, with your permission, I've made arrangements for a private meeting under guard."

Mercado's smile held something in reserve. "I should advise my people of the address."

"Certainly."

The limo had three telephones in back and one up front for the driver. Rodriguez chose the ivory receiver, nestled in between the gold and silver, passing it to his companion as he quoted the address in Medellín. Mercado made his call, arranging for a dozen guns to meet them on the street outside.

It was a mere precaution, just in case Rodriguez and Costanza might have planned a double cross while he was gone. If they were very late, or failed to show at all, his soldiers would disperse and gather reinforcements on their way to slaughter every man, woman and child in the Rodriguez syndicate. Blood retribution for betrayal was the only code Mercado understood or recognized.

Rodriguez didn't mind. He had no hidden aces up his sleeve—not yet—and he wouldn't betray Mercado while their greater enemy was still alive, still threatening to crush them both. It was a matter of priority, Costanza's threat eclipsing every other problem in the dealer's life, demanding an immediate reaction.

It was a twenty-minute drive to Medellín, the scout car leading, chase car bringing up the rear. If anybody tried to stop them, they'd have to deal with gunners fore and aft, plus weapons in the limousine itself. Besides the bodyguards, Rodriguez kept two riot shotguns and an Uzi submachine gun in a secret stash beneath his seat, all primed and ready if the need arose. The limousine was guaranteed to keep on rolling through the concentrated fire of .50-caliber machine guns, even if the heavy-duty tires were blown away. There were hidden gunports spaced around the passenger compartment, letting occupants return fire without emerging from the car.

The vehicle had cost $157,000, but it was nothing to a man of Rodriguez's wealth.

"I have a plan," Mercado announced halfway through the journey, "but it's dangerous."

Rodriguez felt like saying, "Nothing ventured, nothing gained," but he restrained himself and waited, listening.

"The Israelis," Mercado said at last. "They have Costanza's trust."

"Because he knows that they are loyal," Rodriguez countered.

"Are they? I believe we could persuade them to betray him for a price."

"Perhaps."

"The one-eyed man, Auerbach, is still in Panama. If you agree, I'll approach him with an offer that should see the business done."

"How much?"

"Two million dollars for Costanza's head."

Rodriguez blinked, not at the price, but at the thought that it could be so easy. Something told him there had to be a problem with the plan, some crucial flaw, but it would cost them nothing to approach the Israelis and see. If Auerbach or his compatriot took the news back to Costanza, well, it still might be a victory of sorts. Their enemy would see they were determined to destroy him, and his confidence would suffer in the face of their resolve.

"And in the meantime?" he inquired.

"We keep the pressure on, repay Costanza's insults when and where we can. Distract him while his execution is arranged."

"Two million dollars?" He knew that half of it would have to come from him.

Mercado smiled. "As the Americans would say, it would be cheap at half the price."

COSTANZA LISTENED to the gruff voice on the telephone, reciting details of the raid against Trans-Global's training school outside of Medellín. No strangers had been found among the fifteen dead, which meant his enemies had come and gone unscathed, or else had carried off their wounded to a safer place.

The loss of life didn't upset Costanza. Equal numbers would be killed in Medellín on any given day year-round, and he'd long since grown inured to violent death. Exposure of the training camp was troublesome—the damn police would occupy it now undoubtedly—but he'd find another place to educate his *sicarios*. Establishment of the facility was Auerbach's concern, in any case; Costanza merely paid the bills.

It was the sheet audacity of the attack that made him furious, the anger welling up inside until his face flushed scarlet and he felt the heat beneath his skin, a fever that would eat him up alive unless he found some way to vent his rage.

Who dared to challenge him this way, and in his own backyard?

It hadn't been the military or police, that much was certain. Uniforms had reached the scene too late, and from their statements to the press it was apparent that the officers felt cheated of an opportunity to raid the school themselves. Not that its function was a secret from the high command, by any means, but they were duty bound to make a show of ignorance, thereby avoiding explanation of the bribes that had protected the facility for eighteen months.

If not police, then it could only be one of Costanza's various competitors. In essence, that would mean Rodriguez or Mercado, since the other fish were much too small and timid to attempt such an aggressive move.

Rodriguez or Mercado—possibly a combination of the two.

Costanza issued orders, waiting for acknowledgment before he cradled the receiver. He reached for the glass of whiskey he'd placed beside the telephone. Before he made another move, he'd be certain of his targets, making every necessary preparation to destroy them in a single stroke.

Rodriguez and Mercado. Still . . .

He was aware of yesterday's events in Medellín. The raid against a downtown bank had cost Rodriguez several million dollars, much of that discarded in the street like so much trash, the peasants scuffling to claim it like a mob of children grabbing candy under a piñata. The attack on Mercado's nightclub had come hours later, two men shot and killed, extensive damage caused by fire.

Was there a common link between the incidents?

Costanza knew *he* wasn't responsible for yesterday's assaults, but who else would Rodriguez and Mercado naturally suspect? Had one or both of them attacked the training camp in an attempt to even up the score? Could he persuade them of his innocence in time to block an all-out shooting war, and was it even worth his time to try?

Above all else, who was responsible for the attacks against Rodriguez and Mercado? Was it possible the same unknown assailants had destroyed his training camp?

Costanza sipped his drink and frowned, distracted by the prospect of an unknown enemy at large in Medellín. He thrived on power and control, relying on his countless eyes and ears throughout Colombia and the United States to keep him well informed, apprised of any danger in the embryonic stage. If strangers could invade his own hometown, wreak havoc in the streets without a hint of warning, it could only mean there was something seriously wrong, a gap in his security that he'd have to plug at once before the damage spread.

Reviewing the report of a survivor from the camp, he knew that two men had arrived by limousine that morning, talked their way inside the fence, then proceeded to annihilate the staff and students, touching off explosives in the office and destroying crucial records in the fire. Their vehicle—a rental—had been found outside Medellín and traced back to its source where urgent questions had produced a rental contract signed by "Arnold Gresham."

It would be an alias, of course, and probably untraceable, although his men would still be sent to grill the registration clerks in various hotels. Descriptions of the stranger made him relatively short, dark-haired, perhaps Hispanic or Italian. His companion in the limousine had been well dressed, a larger man who looked American.

A tall American, with a Hispanic or Italian at his side. Costanza made a sour face, considering the possibilities and wondering precisely who, in the United States, might wish to see him dead.

The problem was, he had too many suspects. In the past ten years Colombian cartels had undercut the Mafia, the Cubans and assorted other gangs to dominate the cocaine traffic in America. There had been deaths along the way, concessions forced at gunpoint from the kind of men who carried grudges to their graves. If he was forced to make a list of every criminal and dealer in the States who hated him, Costanza could have filled several pages, and they all had eager troops on call to handle any wet work that arose.

It was unlike the Mafia to take their wars outside the United States, but every capo in the country was aware of the outlandish profits in cocaine. Two billion dollars would be worth the risk, a yearly haul that dwarfed La Cosa Nostra's take from gambling and prostitution combined. And if the mafiosi were prepared for war, the goddamn Cubans would be champing at the bit, small-timers hungry for a chance to prove their own machismo as they made a bid for free rides on the gravy train.

But it wouldn't come cheap. That much Costanza promised.

He couldn't point a finger at his enemies so far, but once the culprits were identified, he knew exactly how to deal with them. The recipe remained unaltered from the days when he was a streetwise punk, still wet behind the ears. A challenge—any challenge—must be answered, overcome by force, the challenger eliminated like an insect or a speck of filth. Destruction of one enemy might not prevent another from attacking someday, but it would give the others pause, remind them of the risks inherent in contesting their superiors.

Costanza still had one more call to make. He had to get in touch with Auerbach and brief him on the problem, make arrangements for another training camp to be set up without delay. If they were looking at a war, he'd have need of seasoned troops, and his *sicarios* would all be working overtime.

Costanza frowned and changed his mind. *Two* calls. The best place to discover whether there was Mafia involvement in the recent troubles would be Florida, where La Araña had succeeded in establishing covert connections with the local Family and the police. Inquiries could be made, and by the time another day had passed, he should know something that could be used to single out his enemies and bring them down.

Whoever they might be, the bastards wouldn't find him unprepared.

THE SNATCH HAD GONE like clockwork, and the mark—a second-string lieutenant in the distribution end of the Rodriguez syndicate—had startled them by spilling everything he knew at once before Grimaldi had to shake him down.

Rodriguez and Mercado had arranged their tête-á-tête with maximum security in mind in a sixth-floor office on the fringe of downtown Medellín, with guards downstairs and others in the waiting room outside. Across the street a seven-story building gave the Executioner his altitude and angle of attack, but he'd have to keep his fingers crossed about the rest of it.

Grimaldi parked below, the lot nearly empty after closing time, and kept the engine running for a ready getaway. Decked out in coveralls with the Beretta underneath, Bolan thought he could pass for maintenance if no one stopped him on his way up to the roof and tried to hold an in-depth conversation in the native tongue.

The warrior rode the elevator up alone and took a flight of service stairs to the roof. He moved directly to the western parapet above the street and fixed the target at a range of sixty yards.

Bright lights and silhouettes—as he'd hoped, they hadn't bothered to pull down the blinds.

He knelt and opened up the toolbox, skillfully assembling the Weatherby Mark V. The rifle measured 46.5 inches overall, tipping the scales at close to thirteen pounds when it was loaded, with the twenty-power Redfield scope attached. The magazine would only hold two rounds, with one more up the spout, but it would get him started, and he had six more lined up beside him on the deck.

The scope put Bolan in the office with Mercado and Rodriguez, close enough to count the hairs in each man's nose, if he were so inclined. The cross hairs framed each face in turn, the range almost point-blank, but he didn't intend to execute these men. Not yet.

He'd begun to rattle them the day before, it was working, if Mercado's hasty flight from Panama to Medellín was any indication. Tagging them tonight would leave the smaller of Colombia's cartels in momentary chaos, but their deaths would also free Costanza from the questions he must have about his own misfortune at the murder school. Deprived of likely enemies, Costanza would begin to cast about for other candidates, perhaps increasing his security or even skipping out before the Executioner had time to make the sweep complete.

Tonight was practice, of a sort, another chance to turn his enemies against one another, let them do a portion of the dirty work themselves.

He tucked the shooting plugs in place to save his ears and braced the rubber recoil pad against his shoulder, sighting through the scope on a coffee cup that sat between the men, untouched. Allowing fractions of an inch for parabolic rise at sixty yards, he further compensated for the plate-glass window that would jar his first round out of line. It didn't really matter if he hit the coffee cup or not, but it was something he could fix on, safely in between Rodriguez and Mercado, reasonably certain neither one of them would catch a fragment when he fired.

The Executioner filled his lungs, released a portion of the breath and swallowed hard to lock the rest inside. He stroked the trigger, braced to take the massive recoil as the weapon bucked against his shoulder, sticking with the scope to watch 520 grains of hurtling death drill through the glass and bring it down in jagged sheets, a frozen waterfall.

In fact, he nicked the coffee mug and it exploded into dust, the big .460 round continuing to drill the wall directly opposite and startle the hell out of the gunners in the waiting room. He worked the bolt and fired again before

Rodriguez and Mercado had a chance to fully comprehend they were under fire. His second bullet ripped through the conference table like a hammer stroke and peeled a strip of carpet from the floor.

Downrange, his pigeons went to ground, and Bolan let them go. He used his third round on an empty chair and watched it splinter, pitching over backward to the floor as thunder echoed in his brain.

Reloading swiftly, Bolan had the Weatherby on line again as gunners burst into the office, waving pistols at the shattered window, gaping at the wreckage and their fearless leaders huddled on the floor. He took the point man with a round beneath his chin that nearly ripped his head off, spraying those behind him with a burst of crimson.

Number two was reeling back and wiping at his eyes when Bolan slammed a Magnum round between his ribs and swept him off his feet. The others were retreating, one or two directing aimless pistol fire into the darkness, when he lined up number three and dropped him with a crushing round between the shoulder blades. The impact lifted Bolan's target and propelled him through the open doorway.

The rest escaped as he reloaded, and he used the last three rounds to pin them down, demolishing a lamp and gouging fist-sized chunks of hardwood from the corner of a secretary's desk. When he was satisfied, he broke the big game rifle down and stowed it in his toolbox, double-timing down the stairs and listening to doomsday numbers while he waited for the elevator.

"That was loud," Grimaldi told him as he slid into the waiting car.

"You should have heard it on the other end."

"No thanks. You think they got the message?"

"They're getting there."

13

The frag grenade was fitted with a short three-second fuse. Blancanales put his arm behind the pitch, already counting down when he released the lethal egg. He was huddled in the cover of an outdoor air-conditioning compressor unit when the detonation cleared out half the windows of the small apartment in a spray of shattered glass.

The echoes of the blast were ringing in his skull as Politician scooped up his Uzi and rushed the numbered door. Gadgets and Lyons were there ahead of him, crashing into the smoky interior and firing from the hip.

A sudden thought flashed through Pol's mind—suppose they had the wrong apartment?

No way.

The tip had come through Lyons, from Maria Teresina, though Ironman hadn't told her how he planned to use the information. She'd supplied a list of names and numbers for the major dealers in the area, presumably allowing "Lewis" to coordinate his search for rotten apples in the local DEA. Instead, the names were posted at the head of Able's hit parade, in hopes that three or four selective strikes would shake things loose and spark a chain reaction in the drug community.

The flat on southwest Twenty-eighth was listed as a distribution point for crack and other contraband, but they'd taken time to double-check Maria's information, just in case. The occupants were apparently Colombians, their visitors a random mix of Cubans, blacks and not-so-poor white trash who earned their keep from chemical-free enterprise. A thirty-minute stakeout had been all Politician needed to confirm Maria's listing of the address as a major drug pad on Miami's southwest side.

He crossed the threshold just in time to see Carl Lyons finish off the last of the Colombians, a fat slug of a man who wore his GI .45 inverted in a shoulder rig that left the muzzle buried in the thick bush underneath his arm. The man never had the chance to draw as Lyons hit him with a rising burst that stitched him from his inseam to his double chins and slammed him back against the nearest wall with force enough to dent the plaster. As he slumped to the floor, the dealer looked a bit like Humpty-Dumpty, spilling out his inner secrets on a carpet that would never be the same again.

They checked the bedrooms, just in case, and finally decided not to torch the place, in deference to the neighbors who might suffer damage while they waited for the fire trucks to arrive. It was enough to scatter the cocaine and grind it under foot, a little something for the Metro-Dade forensics team to contemplate—and for the narcs to gnash their teeth about, if some of them had been paid off to look the other way.

"One down," Schwarz announced when they were back inside the car and rolling.

"And four to go," Politician added.

"When word gets around," Lyons offered, "some of them may split before we have a chance to say hello."

"No sweat. We're after ripples, not a perfect sweep."

"I don't like doing things halfway."

"I'll make a note."

"Note this."

"Your girlfriend's bound to have some questions," Gadgets said, "when she turns on the TV tomorrow and starts adding two plus two."

"I'll shine it on. These suckers hit each other all the time. Don't worry."

"*I'm* not worried," Schwarz replied, "but, then again, I haven't got an image to protect."

"Did anybody ever tell you that no one likes a funny Fed?"

"I think you might have mentioned it one time."

"Well, there you are."

"Who's number two?" Politician asked.

"You want to take Ramirez?"

"Might as well. I wouldn't want the guy to feel left out."

Ismael Ramirez was a wheel in North Miami Beach, reportedly connected to the big cartels by blood and marriage, moving major weight among celebrities and businessmen, with tourists as a sideline. The DEA had been "observing" him for twenty-seven months, but they had yet to build a case that would survive judicial scrutiny. They guy was sharp, employing several buffers every time he made a move, and there was nothing to suggest he'd touched an ounce of coke himself since he was popped for snorting at a party back in 1985. The narcs at Metro-Dade suspected him of six or seven homicides, and while Ramirez didn't rank up there with La Araña, he was still a heavy in his own right, worthy of attention while the team had time to kill.

The dealer's home base was a town house one block east of Biscayne Boulevard. He had security in place—two shooters sitting in a car out front, another lounging in some shadows near the door—but it was no big deal to spot them on a drive-by.

"Don't want to wake the neighbors up," Ironman said after parking the vehicle and removing his Colt Python from its shoulder rig in favor of a sleek Beretta 92-F with a silencer attached.

Beside him Schwarz was threading a suppressor onto the muzzle of his Ingram, snapping in a brand-new magazine.

Blancanales took the time to fix a similar customized attachment on his Uzi. With their special parabellum loads, the sound suppression would be relatively uniform, but they couldn't expect their adversaries to respond in kind.

"I'd give it ninety seconds, in and out," Lyons said.

"Fair enough," Schwarz answered, "but I'd like to shave it if we can. The squad cars won't have far to go once someone phones it in."

"All set?" Lyons glanced at Blancanales.

"Ready as I'll ever be."

"Let's do it, then."

They hung together on the short walk back, dividing for the last half block. Pol took the curb side of the stakeout car, his Uzi set for semiautomatic fire, while Lyons slipped around the driver's side. Behind them Gadgets was already drifting toward the town house, ready to eliminate the doorman while they took the two guns in the car.

It went like clockwork, with the shooters sitting there and smoking, windows down, convinced they didn't have a problem in the world. Lyons tagged the driver with a single round behind one ear, the impact slamming him against the steering wheel. Blancanales took the shotgun rider with a quick one-two that spread his brains across the dash. A coughing sound behind them marked the doorman's passing to another plane. Gadgets had the porch staked out as they approached like silent death about to make a house call.

"Back door?" Politician asked.

Lyons shook his head. "With a place like this you either use the front door or you vault the balcony. Unless we dick around, we've got him cold."

"Civilians?"

"Keep your eyes peeled. He's a bachelor, but he might have something soft around the place. You see a woman acting like a soldier, take her out."

"Who wants to knock?"

"And spoil their dinner?" Gadgets asked. "Let's not be rude."

That said, he raised his Ingram with the bulky silencer attached, and fired a point-blank burst into the front door's lock. They were halfway to the den before the opposition showed itself. Two gunners in their shirtsleeves came out of nowhere, following the sound of Schwarz's bullets ripping through the door. One of them had time to shout a warning to his pals before the guns went off.

It wasn't any contest—three on two, with choppers facing pistols—and the two Colombians went down together, twitching arms and legs tangled in a last embrace. They didn't have a chance to use their side arms, but it hardly mattered, since the one guy's dying shout had roused the house.

Upstairs, a rush of feet meant that reinforcements were on the way. Gadgets pressed himself against the inside wall, with Lyons and Pol close behind. Their adversaries opened up with riot shotguns, sight unseen, the buckshot charges ripping holes the size of dinner plates through flimsy stucco walls. A neighbor screamed next door, but Schwarz was busy fighting for his life as two more shooters suddenly appeared downstairs, arriving from the general direction of the dining room.

He caught the point man with a figure eight that dropped him in his tracks before he had an opportunity to use his AK-47. Number two was fading back and pumping wild rounds from a .45 when Lyons gave him two from the Beretta and he went down on his face.

The guys upstairs went wild, their shotguns blasting furniture and shadows, anything at all to make a splash. An M-16 had joined them now, and it was ripping up the walls like a demented chain saw, caring less about effect than sound and fury.

Gadgets palmed a frag grenade and held it for a second after he'd yanked the pin, ensuring it wouldn't have time to tumble back on top of them. The pitch was up and over, simple, but the hostile gunners saw it coming and they opened up with everything they had.

Not good enough.

All three were down, dead or dying by the time Schwarz made the stairs. He vaulted over bodies twisted into shapes their skeletons weren't constructed to accommodate, and someone in the nearest bedroom nearly took his head off with a burst of automatic fire.

The guy was nervous, firing high, or he probably would have scored a kill. Schwarz hit the carpet with his Ingram tracking, spitting fire and parabellum manglers toward the open doorway, hearing Lyons and Pol open up on cue.

It lasted three, four seconds, tops. The shooter panicked, diving for a window with Ironman close behind him, the Beretta chugging twice to close his show. They were already out of time, but there was one more room to check before they swept downstairs, and this time Gadgets let Lyons lead.

They found Ismael Ramirez in the master bedroom, crouching in the middle of a king-size water bed, stripped down to satin boxer shorts. The girl he held in front of him was wearing even less, and there was crazy panic in her eyes, the muzzle of a bright chrome automatic tucked inside her ear.

"Come any closer and I waste the bitch!" Ramirez challenged, slurring part of it from drugs or alcohol, deluded into thinking that a rival hit team would be moved by one more person's death.

"I don't believe you want to do that," Lyons said.

"Fuck you! You psychic, man, or what?"

"I know your future if you drop that hammer on the girl."

"You want her?" There was something dangerous and crazy in the dealer's eyes. "Okay, she's yours."

Ramirez shoved the naked woman toward them, squeezing off two rounds between her shoulder blades and cackling like a lunatic, the automatic rising, looking for another target.

They hit him all at once, the silenced parabellums ripping into him and loosing geysers from the water bed. Ramirez tried to scream, but he was having trouble with his mangled throat, blood choking off his voice, and in another heartbeat he was long past caring, either way. The men of Able left Ramirez floating in a pond of bloody water as the bed deflated, leaking washed-out crimson on the floor.

THIS TIME, Schwarz told himself, they needed more precision. Nailing down a party house was bad enough. They couldn't afford a general massacre with "innocent" civilians tagged and bagged.

"We need a drive-by," Gadgets told Ironman as they rolled down Ninety-fifth Street toward the next target.

"You're telling me?"

"Just making sure."

"No problem. Coming up, the third house on our left."

"I was afraid of that."

He counted five cars in the driveway, and the curb was full on either side. They wouldn't all be in the party house, of course, but even if you figured half...

"I'll bet the neighbors love this place," Pol said.

"Let's try the back."

An alley ran behind the stylish houses to accommodate their garbage cans and keep them off the curb out front. Lyons counted gates and houses, then pulled up behind their destination. A pulse of music reached their ears, and when they stepped outside to peer across the simple wooden fence, they had a glimpse of couples dancing on the patio.

"Selective fire," Schwarz said. "We don't need dead civilians on the evening news."

"You want to tell the other guys?" Lyons asked.

"Tell them nothing," Pol growled. "Just take them down before they have a chance to ask."

They scaled the fence and crossed the yard three abreast, the music reaching out to them and pulling them along. The dancers on the patio ignored them, grooving on one another and the chemicals they'd already pumped into their bloodstreams. Schwarz decided most of them wouldn't have noticed if a tank had rolled across the lawn.

The sliding doors were open and they stepped inside. Behind the bar a slender black man in a velvet sport coat saw them, froze, then made a grab beneath the counter. Lyons shot him once from twenty feet away, the bullet ripping through a cheek and spattering the wall behind him with a crimson mist.

One of the ladies in the living room was winding up to scream, a breathless panting movement that made her look as if she was hyperventilating. Well before she got it out, a pair of strong-arms made their entrance from the kitchen, reaching for their weapons as they cleared the swing doors and made the situation at a glance.

On semiauto Gadgets gave the hulking blonde three rounds and watched him fall, his partner slumping back against the wall as Blancanales shot him in the chest.

Three down, but they were bought-and-paid-for muscle, simply putting in their time. The man in charge was nowhere to be seen, until they crashed the den and caught him on the telephone.

"Hey, what do you—"

A parabellum round burned through the oval of his lips and snapped his head back, swivel chair and all pitched over backward in a heap, the desk phone slithering on top of him. Schwarz moved around the desk and picked up the receiver as an angry voice demanded, "Ziggy? Cut the shit now, will you? Damn it!"

"You've been disconnected," Schwarz said. "Hang on a sec, and you can talk to the police."

The line went dead, and Gadgets punched up 911. The operator sounded bored until he said, "We need a shooting team at— What's the address here?" Lyons told him, and he played it back, ignoring the requests for him to leave his name. "You've got narcotics on the premises and four men dead. Forget about the name game, sugar. I don't have the time to play."

The ripples from their contact in the house had reached the patio as they emerged, a couple of the women squealing while a bodybuilder type with gold chains around his neck moved up to intercept. His hands were empty and his eyes were stoned, but clarity returned as he made out the weapons leveled at his face. "Hey, guys, it's cool!"

"You think so?"

Gadgets caught him underneath the short ribs with a looping right that brought the bodybuilder's dinner back in living color, puddled at his feet before he splashed down onto his knees.

"You done?" Ironman asked him, covering the crowd while Blancanales made a beeline for the fence and waiting car.

Schwarz looked around at frightened, angry faces, raised his Ingram and put the stereo to sleep.

"Okay," he announced, "I'm done."

"THREE OUT OF FIVE'S not bad," Lyons said as he snugged the Python in its shoulder rig and wrapped the silencer-equipped Beretta in a chamois cloth for later cleaning.

"Figure someone tipped the other two?" Blancanales asked.

"Maybe, or they might've just been out. You can't have everything."

"I'd like to try it once."

"Dream on."

"You're stopping by to see Maria?" Gadgets asked.

"In a half hour, give or take."

"Late hours for a working man."

Ironman forced a smile he didn't feel. "When I need a mother-type, I'll let you know."

"You trust the lady, Carl?"

"Is there some reason why I shouldn't?"

Blancanales shrugged. "Survival maybe. You've known her what . . . one day?"

"She fixed us up all right with names."

"She didn't know what she was doing. If she scopes it out, the whole damn thing could blow up in your face."

"I think she'd had it, playing by the rules."

"You sound like you're recruiting, man."

"Get serious. I'm not about to tell her anything she doesn't need to know."

"Be careful with that pillow talk."

"You jealous, Pol?"

"Let's say I'd hate to see you out there on a limb and someone coming up behind you with a power saw."

"If there's a message here, why don't you spit it out?"

"Be careful. That's the message, okay? We're in too deep to have you screwing up our action."

"When's the last time I left anybody hanging, can you tell me that?"

"You never have," Schwarz said. "I wouldn't want to see you break your record."

"Put your mind at ease, okay?"

"If you say so."

"That's the way it is."

He walked his anger off before he reached the car, relaxing as he slid behind the wheel. The guys meant well, he knew that, even if they came off sounding like a pair of constipated mother hens. Besides, they had a point—he *hadn't* known Maria very long, but that wasn't to say he didn't know her well.

The lady was a fighter, a survivor, and he had a feeling she'd understand what they were trying to accomplish in Miami. How she might react was something else, but Lyons didn't plan on forcing a decision. There was no point in confusing her and jeopardizing all they'd worked for when he could rely on his cover with the DEA and keep on milking her for targets in the meantime.

Still, they'd come no closer to their goal of tagging La Araña, shutting down the main cartel connection in South Florida. It might be early days, but Lyons felt each moment slipping through his fingers, wishing there was some way he could make time stand still.

It was entirely possible that their target might not grace Maria's list of dealers in the area. If La Araña was the cold, efficient dude they'd been cautioned to expect, it stood to reason that assorted lesser contacts might not even know his name—much less a lady who was taking on the syndicate without official sanction.

Lyons knew it could still go either way, but in the meantime they were making inroads on the local dealerships. Three targets down, and they could start again tomorrow from the top.

He parked and locked the car, decided not to check his watch before he rang Maria's bell. He wasn't tired, by any means, and she'd asked him to come by regardless of the hour. When she answered, plainly wearing nothing underneath a terry robe, Ironman felt a burst of brand-new energy.

"You're just in time," Maria said.

"For what?"

"Come here and I'll show you."

14

The safehouse was an isolated bungalow on the outskirts of Panama City, maintained by the security police for cases that required a measure of discretion. From the street it looked like any other middle-class abode, but Katz knew there were soundproof rooms inside used for tough interrogations, plus an armory and living quarters for the people in residence.

The one thing he couldn't be sure of was McCarter's actual location in the comfy-looking jail.

Alarms had started going off when the Briton was an hour late returning from his meet with Captain Pablo Arevalo, picking up supposed evidence that would facilitate—or mitigate—a move against Caseros in the days to come. A second hour passed before they got the word of Arevalo's death in a downtown hotel. Katz had put out feelers through the underground, alert to any word of an "unusual" killing or arrest. By midnight they had gotten word—a "British spy" was being questioned by authorities at a secure location, and the names of his accomplices would soon be known.

Katz knew McCarter could be trusted to withstand interrogation for a while, but no one could resist indefinitely, and the use of chemicals eliminated guesswork on the part of the inquisitors. Brute force was easier to get around despite the pain involved, and Katz was hoping the Caseros hit team didn't have a doctor on their staff. If they were simply working McCarter over with a shock baton or rubber hose, there was a decent chance that Phoenix Force could lift him out before their mission in Panama was compromised.

The gruff Israeli knew he was thinking like a combat soldier rather than a friend, but it was fitting given the circumstances. If McCarter had been on the outside of the lockup looking in, he'd have felt the same.

He glanced along the street and saw Gary Manning on the nearest corner, huddled in his trench coat with an automatic rifle underneath. The others would be covering the rear approach, prepared to move on Katz's signal, striking simultaneously from all sides. They didn't know how many troopers were inside, but that was beside the point. Abandoning McCarter was unthinkable, no matter what the odds.

Katz checked the street again before he slipped the Heckler & Koch MP-5 out from under his coat. He flicked off the submachine gun's safety and double-checked to guarantee a live round in the firing chamber, clamping the weapon under his arm as he fished a compact walkie-talkie from his pocket. He pressed the transmitter button with his thumb. "One minute."

Every member of the team was fitted with an earpiece to receive his orders. They also carried radios, but they wouldn't respond except in cases of emergency. Their silence was acknowledgment enough.

Katz glanced downrange and caught a final glimpse of Manning as he disappeared behind a hedge, proceeding toward the eastern corner of the house. He had a window marked for access to the house, provided he got that far, while Katzenelenbogen claimed the front door for himself.

Ten seconds passed before he crossed the street and climbed the waist-high wrought-iron fence. The gate could have been left unoiled deliberately to warn a lookout of approaching strangers, but he doubted whether the Caseros team had given any thought to pressure sensors, trip wires or the like.

The lawn was ankle-high, but Katz ignored the rustling of mice around his feet, eyes locked on the lighted windows of the house. The soundproof rooms would be inside somewhere, removed from easy access to the outer world, but he'd have to pass the sentries first. And if they tried to stop him . . .

Katz smiled. Resistance was the one thing he could count on. That, and the minute advantage of surprise.

By 4:13 A.M. McCarter had begun to classify the different kinds of pain. He started with the throbbing in his skull where someone had applied his pistol butt before they'd taken him into custody. It was a different sort of pain than the pulsing in his battered face, although the two sensations merged somewhere behind his eyes, becoming one. The burning of an open cut below one eye was different yet, and none of the above bore any similarity to the persistent aching of his ribs.

So far the hit team had been satisfied with fists and boots, but they were getting tired and were discussing variations on the theme. McCarter hadn't told them anything, although he understood their questions well enough, not even name and rank, much less the details of his mission or the presence of his four associates in Panama.

The question was, how long could he hold out?

His tormentors were whispering among themselves, but the Briton heard enough of the conversation to know they were talking electricity. He knew the tricks, had seen them used, and understood that it would be a different game once they attached electrodes to his genitals. He could perhaps delay the worst of it by making up stories, inviting them to check out his information, but in the end they'd discover he was lying and return to finish off the job.

By now the others would be searching high and low for him, which was small comfort in a foreign city where their contacts were considered unreliable at best. It might be days before they found him—if they ever did—and in the meantime every moment brought McCarter closer to a breakdown that would jeopardize his mission and his friends.

The SAS had trained him for a situation such as this, assuming that a member of the team might one day fall into the hands of terrorists. It hadn't happened yet, as far as McCarter knew, but the security police employed by General Caseros were the next best thing to the PLO or the IRA—assassins with authority to maim and torture as they pleased as long as they stood fast behind their president.

If he could only reach a weapon . . . then, what?

There were three men with him in the soundproof room, and six or seven others he knew about throughout the house. There could be others. Nine men at least, and even if they put a pistol in his hand . . .

McCarter fixed on the alternative, the only ironclad guarantee of silence, and his mind rebelled. Not yet. Persuade them he had to use the toilet, anything at all to make them loosen the bonds that held his wrists in place behind his back. A momentary lapse, and he could grab the nearest gunner, reach his holster—make them kill him, if it came to that, but go out fighting like a man.

The worst part of captivity was feeling helpless. It was always easier to take a beating on your feet when you could strike back at your enemies, however ineffectually. A part of it was simple pride, the rest wrapped up in all the mumbo jumbo of psychology, but it boiled down to power versus impotence. A captive mind gave up before the body went and thereby made things easy for enemy.

One of his keepers disappeared—door open, closed—and came back moments later with an odd contraption that resembled something from the early days of telephone communication. A hand crank stuck out of the left side of a metal box, with dangling wires and shiny alligator clips where McCarter thought the earpiece ought to be.

It was a simple generator that would charge your battery or singe your flesh, depending on the job at hand. Simplicity itself, and still light-years beyond brass knuckles or a rubber hose.

McCarter still wore slacks and shoes, although his shirt had been removed upon arrival so that the inquisitors could snuff out their cigarettes on his chest. If they removed his pants—and what else could they have in mind?—he thought they might be forced to free his hands, however briefly, to facilitate the move. Anticipating freedom, he began to flex his fingers, bringing back what circulation he could manage in defiance of his bonds.

In the end they cheated him, unfastening his belt and pulling down his zipper, roughly lowering the slacks and shorts around his knees before they started on his shoes. It *was* required to free his ankles first before the team could finish stripping him, and in his sudden desperation he decided, *What the hell?*

The soldier on his left was careless, freeing McCarter's leg and staying close enough to make a ready target as the Briton raised his foot and slammed his naked heel against the trooper's nose. It cost him, fists and truncheons raining down on his head and shoulders, battering his chest and ribs, but it was worth it.

In the flash before they beat him into semiconsciousness, McCarter saw his adversary stretched out on the floor, blood pumping from his flattened nostrils.

A little something for the bastards to remember when they finished with him, dumping him wherever they deposited their throwaways. Not much, but it was all he had to give.

In contrast to the ringing in his skull, the alligator clips felt small and distant, barely pinching him at all. If that lot was the worst they could do...

But he was wrong, and in the moment when he recognized his critical mistake, Carter found the strength to scream.

AT HOME IN DARKNESS Calvin James approached the target house and took up his position, waiting for the second hand of his watch to signal the attack. In front of him was a door that offered access to the kitchen and three Hispanics who sat at a table while a bottle made the rounds.

Another fifteen seconds.

James had opted for the CAR-15, a 40 mm M-203 launcher mounted underneath the barrel and a buckshot round in place. The door was locked, of course—it had to be in a place like this—but if the strike went down on time, James thought he'd have an edge.

Five seconds.

Stepping back a pace for spread, he checked the window one more time to put his mind at ease. Not bulletproof. Cheap bastards poured their whole damn budget into rigging up interrogation rooms and hardly gave a thought to their exterior security. The arrogance of power made them think that no one in his right mind would attempt to interfere.

"Could be you got that right," James told the darkness, shouldering his weapon as the time ran out.

He fired the launcher, shattering the window with a blast of double-aught that swept the table end to end. Already moving as the echo died, James hit the door latch with a 3-round burst and kicked his way inside to find his human targets writhing on the floor.

Correction. Two of them were writhing, clutching chest and gut wounds, but the third was clearly out of it, a grisly clot of bone and tissue where his head should have been.

James finished off the other two with mercy rounds and kept it moving, picking up on sounds of violent conflict in adjoining rooms as other members of the team made their plays.

McCarter might be dead already, Calvin knew, but kicking ass came first. It was the only way he knew to play the game.

THE THOUGHT of torture took Rafael Encizo back to his experience with Castro's jailers at El Principe Prison, and it brought a flush of anger to his face. At one point in his life he'd believed that killing Communists was all it took to liberate the world, but he'd learned a thing or two since then.

For instance, he'd come to realize that violence had no politics. It was a tool, for good or evil, all depending on the way it was applied. Some men took life or maimed their fellowmen to keep a fragile grip on power that would slip away someday no matter what they did or who they killed along the way. It didn't matter in the long run if the killers posed as Communists or fascists, right-wing vigilantes or warriors of "national liberation." If their hearts were rotten, everything they did or tried to do was done for evil's sake.

The flip side of the coin consisted of the chosen few who used their martial skills to make a difference, countering the savages and surgically removing the malignancies that threatened civilized society. Most soldiers and policemen served their tours of duty in a kind of trance, expecting trouble, never really thinking it would be their turn to kill— or die. The chosen few made life-and-death decisions every day and were compelled to act on the choices they made.

Like now.

Inside the house, one friend and an uncertain number of the enemy. The task of helping one and wiping out the rest would be a challenge, but Encizo was prepared to give it everything he had.

Beginning with his entry into the house.

The sliding doors were glass, designed in California style to give the residents a view of flower gardens that had long since gone to seed. The draperies were drawn halfheartedly, but there was ample room for Encizo to peer inside and see two men reclining on a couch. There might be others in the room—he couldn't tell—but it would make no difference. He was going in on cue regardless, and the men who tried to stop him were as good as dead.

The flowerpot was inspiration, large enough to do the job yet light enough that it wouldn't throw Encizo completely off his stride. A simple pitch and follow-through in force should do the trick, and if he lost it at the final instant, found himself outnumbered and outgunned, at least he would have done his best.

He flicked the safety off his Uzi, hanging on a strap around his neck, and weighed the flowerpot in one hand, waiting. At the proper moment he stepped forward, putting all his weight behind the toss, advancing in a crouch as glass exploded.

Encizo cleared the threshold with a diving shoulder roll and came up with the Uzi in his hands, a stream of parabellums hacking right to left across the sofa. From the expressions on their faces neither one of his intended targets understood precisely what was happening. They twitched and died without a chance to reach their guns.

Not so the other two, unseen before he'd burst into the room. One of them stood before a built-in bookcase stacked with paperbacks and girlie magazines, a dog-eared *Penthouse* in his hands and disbelief etched on his face. The other had been lounging in a canvas chair before Encizo had crashed the party, sipping a can of beer, but he discarded it and drew a bulky automatic, squeezing off a round as the Phoenix fighter swung back to bring them under fire. The bullet whispered past his face, and Encizo triggered a burst that punched the gunman over backward in his chair, feet pointed at the ceiling for an instant, finally going all the way to wind up in a flaccid heap.

The reader dropped his magazine and fumbled for the pistol on his hip. Too late. Encizo caught him with a rising burst that raked him from the knees to collarbone before he crumpled, going down.

Encizo reloaded on the move, the sound of gunfire from adjoining rooms a lure that urged him on. The action wasn't over yet.

He still had work to do.

THE EMPTY ROOM took Gary Manning by surprise. He heard the sounds of combat all around him, but his entry into the safehouse—through a window left unlocked—had gone unnoticed by the enemy. Advancing through the semidarkness of an empty bedroom, he had nearly reached the door when it swung open and a tall Hispanic stood before him, man and submachine gun framed in silhouette.

It was a matter of a heartbeat, give or take, and the Canadian was faster, triggering a short burst from his M-16 that blew the shadow man away. He had a glimpse of crimson teardrops on the wall outside, the prostrate body twitching slightly as he stepped across the threshold to confront another gunman in the corridor.

This time the goon was working with an edge, but nerves made him forget to squeeze the trigger gently, jerking it instead and stitching ragged holes across the stucco wall to Manning's left. One strike was all that was given in the life-or-death league, and the M-16 was spitting back at him before the shooter could correct his aim, the 5.56 mm tumblers ripping through his chest and slamming him against the nearest wall.

The warrior's instinct led Manning toward the center of the house, where the interrogation rooms would be secure from prying eyes. He recognized the soundproof door at once and was advancing when it opened, one of the inquisitors emerging with a broad smile on his face, oblivious to the approach of sudden death.

Of course.

The soundproof insulation worked both ways, which meant the men assigned to grill McCarter didn't know their time was running out.

Another microsecond changed all that. The short Hispanic blinked once at Manning and reached for the automatic he wore inverted in an armpit holster. The Canadian shot him twice and followed through before his body hit the floor, the echoes of his own fire rolling on ahead of him to freeze the startled troopers where they stood.

He had a fleeting glimpse of McCarter, sitting naked in a wooden chair, his arms and legs secured, before it went to hell. The two surviving members of the third-degree team broke in opposite directions, one man reaching for a pistol on his hip, the other diving for a shoulder holster he'd draped across a nearby chair.

Proximity made Manning take the armed man first, a short burst nearly ripping off his head. His sidekick reached the weapon he'd found too cumbersome to wear, but he didn't get an opportunity to use it as the tumblers caught him from behind and clipped his spinal column, slamming him headfirst into a corner of the room.

Now it was time for McCarter, to free his hands and arms, release the alligator clips his interrogators had attached—

Then Manning froze, a Spanish curse behind him nearly covering the sharp sound of a weapon being cocked. His M-16 was on the floor in front of him, both hands extended, empty, toward the shiny alligator clips.

The end.

He saw it in McCarter's eyes, and knew he had to try it, anyhow.

The burst of automatic fire made Manning flinch, somehow aware he was still alive as he scooped up the M-16 and twisted toward the doorway, just in time to see his nameless adversary slump and slither down the jamb. He recognized another figure in the doorway as Katz in the time it took for Manning to release the trigger, sweating as he turned back toward McCarter and the metal jaws that held his flesh.

"Hang in there, eh? We're almost home."

Somehow McCarter found the strength to smile. His voice was cracked and parched from screaming as he answered, "Almost home."

15

Luis Costanza was glancing at his diamond-studded watch when the houseman knocked and stuck his head inside the den. "He's here, sir."

Costanza nodded. "Send him in."

The new arrival was Costanza's second cousin, but any physical resemblance between the two was limited to thick dark hair and their expensive mode of dress. Miguel Costanza was a full head shorter than his relative and heavyset, a man for whom the good life had become a way of going soft.

"You're late, Miguel."

"I must apologize, Luis. The driver thought that we were being followed."

"Were you?"

"I believe he was mistaken. One car seemed to stay with us around the block, but when we made a few more turns..."

The stocky man put on a smile and spread his hands. Luis Costanza felt his anger simmering, but used a neutral tone as he replied. "You know about our troubles, cousin. I won't be pleased if you've shown the enemy where they can come and visit me."

"I'm not a fool, Luis."

His cousin sounded hurt, but it wasn't Costanza's problem. At the moment he had other subjects on his mind. "How long since you've been in touch with La Araña?"

"In Miami?" He asked the question as if there were another lurking somewhere close at hand. "Two weeks, I think. Perhaps a little more."

"It's time for you to make another call."

"As you think best."

"I need to know if the Italians are behind the recent difficulties, or if there's someone else—a stranger from America—who wants to harm our family."

"The government perhaps?"

It was a thought that had already crossed Costanza's mind. He frowned and shrugged. "The DEA is bound by rules and regulations, treaties and the like. The White House might send troops, invade the country if their cause was desperate enough . . . but this?"

"The CIA perhaps?"

"Too obvious. Since Watergate they've been forced to work under a microscope."

"A private party, then."

"It's what we must discover. If the Cubans or the Mafia aren't involved, we must take steps to isolate and neutralize our enemy before he goes too far."

"If La Araña has the name?"

"I want a full assessment of potential damage. After that we can protect ourselves by any means required."

"Of course, Luis."

"There's a possibility Rodriguez and Mercado are responsible," Costanza continued. "If so, they must be punished. La Araña will be free to deal with their associates in the United States as necessary to prevent a repetition of disruptive incidents."

Miguel looked vaguely anxious, as he always did when executions were discussed. Costanza couldn't say if it was nerves, or if his cousin longed to take on a portion of the wet work himself. Appearances could be deceiving, after all, and there might be a trace of steel beneath the baby fat, if one looked deep enough.

For his part, though, Costanza didn't plan to test Miguel. If he was right, firsthand experience with bloodshed might inspire his cousin to become ambitious, looking at Costanza's throne with hungry eyes. If he was wrong, Miguel's incompetence and inexperience—worse yet, his weakness—would disgrace the family. In either case it was a no-win proposition, and Costanza meant to keep his cousin on a leash, confined to office chores and other simple tasks where he could earn a living for himself without endangering the business as a whole.

"It shall be done, Luis."

"At once."

"Of course."

Miguel excused himself and left the study. After he'd gone, Costanza lit a cheroot and sat back in his padded swivel chair, eyes closed, examining the possibilities.

In one scenario Rodriguez or Mercado—possibly the two of them together—launched a shooting war against Costanza to devour his territory and the profits he derived from being number one. The theory's major weakness was its failure to explain how both Mercado and Rodriguez were themselves attacked *before* the raiders had fixed Costanza in their sights.

Coincidence? A string of unrelated incidents?

Costanza kept his options open, but he'd begun to search for viable alternatives. A brash fourth party, currently unrecognized, who sought to topple *all* the ranking dealers and combine their action in a kind of supersyndicate? If not the Cubans or the Mafia, perhaps a total stranger, entering the game without an invitation or a notion of his proper place.

What the Americans would call a wild card, driven to extremes by greed that made him risk his life and those of his subordinates.

Another possibility, suggested by Miguel and running far behind the others, was the notion of a covert government assault against Costanza and his chief competitors. He knew the Americans discussed such things—they sometimes even published editorials demanding "frontier justice" in the case of famous fugitives—but talk was far removed from action in the great democracies. The so-called "war on drugs" was ten years old without a major victory for the authorities, and Washington had spent the past twelve months on repetitious studies of the problem, killing time as if the traffic in cocaine had only been discovered on the latest President's inauguration day. It was the longest-running joke Costanza knew, and he couldn't imagine anyone in Washington possessing the guts to confront him like a man.

That left Rodriguez and Mercado, or the wild card. If a stranger was involved, Costanza would be points ahead if he could prove as much to his competitors, before their anger sparked a three-way shooting war in Medellín. Together they could stand united in the face of opposition from outside and settle their private difficulties later when the way was clear.

Cooperation in a crisis might have beneficial side effects, as well. It would be easier to kill Rodriguez and Mercado later, when the time came, if they looked upon Costanza as their friend.

He smiled, reminded that the only way to guarantee security was to eliminate all enemies, however large or small they might appear. There would be others in the months and years ahead, of course, but for the moment he had ample targets for his guns.

The problem was the beginning—where to start and how best to ensure that there were no mistakes, no oversights.

Investigation, first, and he would trust in La Araña to discover any leads in the United States. At home, in Medellín and Bogotá, Costanza had sufficient eyes and ears to do the job.

He'd begin at once and see the business done as rapidly as possible. Before the week was out his enemies would understand the nature of their grave mistake, and it would be too late.

The thought brought laughter to Costanza's lips.

A joke upon his enemies to take them by surprise.

MIGUEL COSTANZA WAS a man who knew his limitations. He had never been a fighter, so he made his way by guile and stealth. It helped to have a cousin like Luis, whose wealth and reputation gave Miguel an aura of vicarious respect. Men might not fear Miguel for who he was, but no one in his right mind tampered with the second cousin of Luis Costanza.

From time to time Miguel imagined what it would be like to deal from strength, intimidating strangers and potential enemies with his reserves of ready cash, the troops at his immediate command.

Someday perhaps. Soon.

Miguel had no idea who was responsible for the attacks on his cousin and the others, but he'd find out—with help from La Araña—and the knowledge would be worth its weight in platinum. It would be a chance to prove himself before Luis.

It troubled him to deal with La Araña, even from a distance, but he had no choice. Luis had given him instructions, and it wouldn't do for him to fail at such a vital task. He'd remind himself about the miles that lay between himself and the killer, and the unlikelihood that they'd ever meet. La Araña was a valued tool, unrivaled when it came to punishment of enemies or the intimidation of competitors. Without the web of terror that La Araña wove across South Florida, with tendrils stretching from the Carolinas into Houston and New Orleans, the Costanza family might never have attained its present dominance in the narcotics trade.

The merchandise sold itself by word of mouth, but there were always other sources and suppliers, men and syndicates prepared to undersell or muscle in at any sign of weakness. A successful merchant needed killers at his beck and call, prepared to act on command without a trace of conscience, and La Araña had no peers among that armed fraternity.

It might be possible, he thought, to use the talents of the family's hired killer to his own advantage, over time, but he'd have to move with caution, using safety measures all the way. Luis would never grasp his full potential as a leader—relatives were always prone to pick and criticize—and it would be Miguel's task to instruct him in the harsh realities of life.

How best to do the job?

It was a riddle, but the answer would present itself in time. One option—if Rodriguez and Mercado were suspected of the raid against the training camp for Luis's youthful hit teams, Miguel might find a way to use their animosity and profit from the coming war. Luis wasn't immortal, after all. A well-placed bullet was enough to do the job, and if a well-known enemy was linked to the assassination . . .

On the other hand, it might be easier to use La Araña, organize a double cross that would *appear* to be the work of devious competitors. Miguel already had connections in Miami; next, he had to test the waters, feel out La Araña on subjects such as loyalty versus profit. If the killer was agreeable, who better to defeat the various security precautions laid on by Luis?

The thought of a decisive move against his cousin caused Miguel to tremble, terror and excitement mingling to send shivers down his spine. Once he was committed to the plan, there would be no reversal, no escape. He'd be open to betrayal, as Luis was every day, and knowing it would make him strong. He would reward the men who served him, punish those who proved disloyal…but first he had to win the game itself.

And what about Ortega, standing on the right hand of the throne, convinced he would rule the roost one day? He was a savage, capable of anything—but he was also just a man. Like any other, he could be deceived, eliminated. Swept away.

No easy talk, regardless of the confidence he felt inside. It would begin with La Araña, but he had to take things slowly, carry out a portion of his cousin's business first before he made his own approach.

A game of wits in which Miguel believed he might surprise his so-called friends and enemies alike. They judged him weak across the board, but he'd prove them wrong. It took a strong man to revolt against the bonds of blood and carve himself a niche among the leading players in his chosen field. To rise above the best, it took a man of strength *and* vision, someone to be reckoned with.

But first the call.

To serve himself he first must serve Luis. There was a certain logic—even symmetry—about the situation that appealed to him and made him smile.

La Araña would know what to do when it was time.

Miguel could wait.

OTHER THAN the company that had installed the telephones, six persons in the world knew La Araña's private number in Miami. In Medellín there was Luis Costanza, Ortega, his second-in-command, and Miguel Costanza. Two of La Araña's chief lieutenants in Miami also had the number, as well as a contact in New Orleans who did business with the Dixie Mafia and state police.

In normal times the private line rang one or twice a week on average. Men who dealt with La Araña typically preferred to wait for orders rather than initiating contact on their own. It made them feel as if the violence touched their lives less intimately somehow, sparing them some measure of the risk involved. Not innocence precisely, but the next best thing.

Emergencies brought calls in greater numbers, and the phone had rung three times that night alone. La Araña's two lieutenants in Miami had reported on a rash of unexpected shootings, ten or fifteen people dead, the gunners unidentified. As luck would have it, all the targets had been working for José Mercado or Raul Rodriguez, dealing merchandise in competition with Costanza's family. It was a situation for La Araña to observe, but nothing that demanded intervention—yet.

The third time it was Miguel.

La Araña answered on the second ring and recognized his voice at once, the question he invariably asked in place of salutations.

"Is the line secure?"

"Of course."

"I'm calling for Luis."

"Is there a problem?"

"Someone moved against the school today—the training camp."

"I understand."

"Luis suspects Rodriguez or Mercado—possibly the two of them together—but he isn't sure."

"Why not?"

"There have been other incidents during the past two days, and we aren't the only targets. Coincidence perhaps, and yet—"

"You told Luis it was *coincidence?*" It was an effort not to laugh out loud.

Sounding hurt, Miguel said, "He didn't ask for my opinion."

That, at least, was wise. "What does he want from me?"

"A name if possible. He's reluctant to proceed without a clear fix on the enemy."

"I understand. But if Rodriguez and Mercado are involved—"

"The gunmen were Americans, or so it seems."

La Araña frowned at the new twist on the game they'd played so many times. "Is that confirmed?"

"Within our limitations at the moment, yes."

It was amusing to the killer to hear Miguel discussing limitations like a man who'd already overcome his own. Another time La Araña might have made some joke or sly remark, but not tonight. "I'll see what I can do."

"One other thing. Luis has asked that you report to me with your results, and no one else."

The last was a transparent lie, but there appeared to be no point in challenging Miguel. If he was cooking up some move against Luis, it would be obvious in time, and at the moment there were other mysteries to solve. "As you prefer."

"I shall look forward to your call."

The line went dead and La Araña cradled the receiver, frowning. An attack upon Luis Costanza in Colombia wasn't exactly unexpected in the current atmosphere of chaos that prevailed. Coordinated strikes against Costanza and his chief competitors, implied by Miguel, were something else entirely. If Rodriguez and Mercado were the targets of attacks in Medellín *and* Miami, it implied a full-scale conflict in the making.

Who would dare to attack all three cartels at once? The prospects for survival—much less victory—were miniscule unless the strike force was supremely organized, well financed, ready for a struggle to the death. La Araña thought about a new cartel and shrugged it off. Costanza would have been the first to know if any of his neighbors had begun to organize and arm themselves for war.

Outsiders, then, with implications of American involvement in Colombia. Considering the Cubans, La Araña ruled them out on principle, convinced from personal experience that they could never mount an international campaign of any consequence.

The Mafia?

It was a fact that the Sicilians had been traumatized by federal prosecutions in the past few years, but several Families still had the strength to wage a decent war, and if a working coalition had been organized . . .

La Araña made a mental note to call New Orleans in the morning, put out feelers to the underground. Around Miami there were also sources to be tapped and information to be gleaned. It seemed impossible that anyone could launch a war of such dimensions without leaving something of himself behind to mark the trail.

And when the culprits were identified, what then?

More choices were to be made, depending on Costanza's prospect of success against the enemy. Above all else, La Araña was a natural survivor, hanging on this long through grim refusal to support the losing side.

There might be changes in the wind, but it was far from certain.

The smell of blood *was* certain, though—and close at hand.

A brand-new day was coming. La Araña smiled in sweet anticipation of the feast.

16

"You promised me security."

"Against a madman? What should I have done?"

José Mercado stared across the broad expanse of desk at Raul Rodriguez, noting the fear combined with anger in the dealer's eyes.

How *could* Rodriguez have anticipated the attack? Would it have made a difference if the blinds were drawn, for instance, or another site had been selected for the meeting?

"I don't know," Mercado replied, a measure of his own rage fading as he spoke.

The room in which they sat was windowless, and a complement of six armed men was deployed outside the single door. Downstairs another dozen sat in cars or loitered on the sidewalk, automatic weapons hidden underneath their jackets. No one could approach *this* meeting place without some warning in advance.

"Costanza?"

Mercado shrugged. With three men freshly killed, they knew no more about their enemy now than they'd known the day before. Costanza was a clear-cut possibility, and yet . . .

"I still have doubts about the camp," Mercado said at last.

"What doubts?"

"I know that I'm not responsible for the attack. You say the same."

"You doubt my word?"

Mercado raised an open hand. "I've said nothing of the kind. But it remains a fact that *someone* moved against Costanza, and if we didn't, then who?"

"Perhaps we should be asking him," Rodriguez suggested.

"Perhaps."

The thought of chatting with Costanza brought a sour taste to Mercado's mouth. He didn't trust the man and hated the idea of going to Costanza like a peasant, hat in hand. If they could speak as equals, one man to another...

"I was thinking," Rodriguez said, "that he might have staged the raid himself."

"But why?"

"Some trouble with the Israelis perhaps. If they demanded more than he was willing to supply..."

Rodriguez left it hanging, for Mercado to complete the picture from his own imagination. It was possible, he thought, but wouldn't it be simpler to eliminate the Israelis themselves without demolishing the camp?

Mercado shook his head. "I don't believe it."

"Then we might be dealing with a stranger. It makes matters worse."

"Or better."

Once again Mercado's mind reviewed the possibilities. If they could reach Costanza and persuade him of a common threat, there was an outside chance he might agree to help them, forge a solid front against the enemy. United they would be invincible, and once the enemy was vanquished... well, it would be easier to trap and kill a "friend" whose guard was down.

But how best to approach Costanza in the present circumstances? He undoubtedly suspected one or both of them in the attack on his murder school. A simple phone call wouldn't do the trick, and there was no way to approach him physically without provoking bloodshed in the streets.

It was a problem, but one Mercado felt he'd ultimately solve. No man was absolutely inaccessible, a fact that had been driven home that very night. This time, however, he wouldn't be looking for a way to kill Costanza. Not just yet.

In short, clipped phrases he explained his plan. Rodriguez scowled, finally nodding like a man who understood he had no viable alternative. It went against the grain to ask their enemy for help—for anything—but the alternative was splitting up their forces, waging war on two fronts simultaneously, both against Costanza and an enemy whom they hadn't, as yet, been able to identify.

And if Luis Costanza *was* responsible for the attacks they had suffered, then they'd know it soon enough. He'd accept their overtures too readily, an enemy too anxious to make friends. Mercado thought he could read Costanza like an open book—or well enough, at least, to save himself.

But first, before they played the game, he had to make another call. "I need to get in touch with Ernesto Ramos in Miami."

"Why?" Rodriguez asked. "How can he assist us?"

"If Costanza turns us down or tries a double cross, I want to be prepared. Ernesto has been tracking La Araña, and I want the bastard neutralized in case of trouble with Luis."

Rodriguez paled at the mention of the Costanza hitter, cursing softly.

"You disagree?"

Reluctantly Rodriguez shook his head. "It must be done, but carefully."

"Of course."

Which meant Rodriguez didn't want to have his name associated with the act. No problem. With La Araña dead Mercado would be more than happy to monopolize the credit for a move that would immeasurably boost his personal prestige.

"The telephone?"

There was none in the room, surprisingly, despite its seeming function as an office. With a frown Rodriguez reached out and pushed a button on his intercom and demanded a telephone be brought to him.

In seconds flat a gunman entered, carrying a desk phone, which he placed on the desk, retreating after he had plugged its long extension cord into a wall jack.

"Shall I . . . ?"

Rodriguez stood, as if to leave the room and give him privacy. Mercado shook his head and waved him back. "Unnecessary. We're friends here, after all."

The "for now" remained unspoken.

A BREATHER, Bolan told himself. No more, no less. His targets needed time to lick their wounds and point accusing fingers before he made another move. Too much, too soon, could blow his act, and there wouldn't be time to start from scratch if anything went wrong.

And while he waited Bolan's mind reached out for home. For Hal.

He used a pay phone and a credit card that billed the call to Mike Belasko, roving troubleshooter for an international petroleum conglomerate. In fact, the bills were routed back to Stony Man Farm, where Barbara Price and Aaron Kurtzman settled the tab. It was a system that had functioned well enough in other combat zones, and while he knew some governments routinely listened in on public telephones, Colombia's near-anarchy wasn't conducive to errant spot surveillance.

Even so, you never knew who might be listening at Brognola's end of the line, and Bolan ran their normal drill to guarantee security. Considering the hour, he punched up Stony Man direct, a relay number that would automatically reroute the call to the big Fed's home. It would be answered on his private line, swept twice a day for taps, and if a trace should be attempted, searchers would discover that the call had terminated with a dial-a-prayer recorder message out of Arlington, Virginia.

Bolan waited through the shunts and switches, with Brognola picking up before the phone could ring a second time.

"Hello?"

"You're sitting on it," Bolan said.

"I brought work home." There was a heartbeat of hesitation at the other end. "You've been a busy boy."

"You heard?"

"We're catching echoes. Nothing hard and fast, but from the gist of it, I gather you've been stirring up a hornet's nest."

"I'm working on it. Any word from other fronts?"

"Miami's heating up," Brognola replied, "but we've got too damn many players in the game down there for me to get a fix this soon. I haven't heard a lot from Phoenix, but you know they're on the job."

A small alarm went off in Bolan's mind. "No problems?"

"If there are, I haven't been advised."

"Katz likes to work things out himself."

"That sounds familiar," the big Fed replied. "I don't suppose you've got a fix on where we're going yet?"

"It's early," Bolan said, reflecting that, in fact, his second day was nearly gone. "I'm giving it a rest tonight to let thing stew."

"It couldn't hurt," Brognola answered, trusting Bolan from experience, his knowledge of the general plan, although he was completely in the dark about specifics. Either way it went, the game in Medellín was Bolan's show.

"I guess that's it." The Executioner was anxious to maintain the contact, but he knew he was only marking time.

"You sure?"

"I'm sure."

"Take care, eh?"

Bolan smiled. "You know me, guy."

"Damn right. Be careful, anyway."

Brognola severed the connection first, and Bolan listened to the dead line humming in his ear for several seconds before returning the receiver to its cradle. On the walk back to his car he sifted through Brognola's words and tried to read between the lines.

Miami heating up.

That meant Able Team had found a target—probably a list of targets—and the battle had been joined. Brognola didn't know if they were close to La Araña yet, or whether they could hold their own against the odds. He wished them well.

The silence out of Panama was even more disturbing than the combat echoes from Miami. Phoenix Force was working behind enemy lines in the shadow of a hostile military government, and any slip could spell disaster with a tyrant like Caseros in the driver's seat. Five men could disappear without a trace if they were fingered by the enemy, and it would be a virtual impossibility to track them down.

Still, Bolan meant what he'd said to Brognola about the gruff Israeli leader's tendency to handle problems on his own without requesting aid from higher up. It was a trait Katz shared in common with the other members of his team, and Bolan knew one thing beyond the shadow of a doubt—if Phoenix bought the farm, they'd be going out with fire and thunder, raising hell enough for Brognola to feel the shock waves back in Wonderland.

With that in mind, the silence might mean they were working on a covert angle of attack, or else that there was simply nothing to report so far. Caseros had been covering his ass in Panama for years, sometimes with the assistance of the CIA, and it defied all logic to expect he'd topple overnight. Ten days was pushing it, for Bolan's money, but he knew Katz would spare no energy to pull it off.

The knowledge didn't put his mind at ease exactly, but the Executioner had seen enough combat that he understood the risks of personal distraction on the firing line. The men of Phoenix Force were seasoned pros, and there was no way he could help them out by sitting in Colombia and worrying about their progress. Conversely the diversion of his full attention just might get him killed—a circumstance that would, in turn, rebound on Phoenix and on Able Team with grim results.

Face forward, then. The warrior knew his enemies, although he couldn't put his finger on the men in charge at any given moment of the day of night. Rodriguez and Mercado would have burrowed deep by now, still shaking from their close encounter with a sniper whose identity remained a point of speculation. Their first reaction, pointing fingers at Costanza, would be tempered by confusion if they stopped and used their heads, considering the fact that each had been attacked within the past two days. It would be Bolan's task to keep them scrambling and guessing while he brought the loose end of his plan together in a noose—and pulled it tight around their necks.

With that in mind the Executioner decided there was no point sitting back and waiting while his enemies gained strength or started adding two and two. He had a list of targets fresh in mind, and there was no time like the present to continue with the game.

He walked back to the phone booth, dropped a coin and dialed Grimaldi's room at the hotel.

"Yeah?"

"You want to take a ride?"

"THAT'S PERFECT, baby, just like that."

Ernesto Ramos crossed both hairy arms behind his head and watched Dolores work, her long hair spilling like a curtain across his groin as her head bobbed up and down. The woman had a magic tongue.

At first he let himself imagine that the jangling telephone was only in his mind, an audio accompaniment to the sensations flaring in his loins. The second ring convinced him otherwise, but Ramos waited through another four, still hoping the caller would give up and go away.

"Hello?"

"Ernesto."

It wasn't a question, and he didn't have to guess about the voice. Mercado. Ramos felt himself begin to wilt. Dolores noted his reaction with surprise and worked harder to regain lost ground, until he sat up in the bed and pushed her away.

"What's happening."

"It's funny you should ask," Mercado said. "I hoped you might tell me."

"We're keeping busy here, you know? Just moving merchandise, is all."

"That's it?"

"You mean that other thing we talked about?"

"You read my mind."

"I'm right on top of it, you bet. We tried to nail it down a couple of days ago, but there were problems. Couple of the guys got sick, you know? I had to lay them off."

"You've got replacements, right?"

"No sweat, boss, it's covered. Only thing is, now I've got to work some angles, try to make the touch with people watching me, you know?"

"If it was easy, anyone could do it."

"Right, I hear you. No excuses. I'm just telling you, it's bound to take a little time."

"We're out of time, Ernesto. Things are breaking here that you don't even want to know about. I need a win to even up the score, you follow me?"

"I hear you loud and clear. Consider it a promise."

"That's exactly what I *do* consider it, Ernesto. I sincerely hope you're not fool enough to make a promise when you can't deliver."

"Me?" The perspiration on his forehead felt like slime, all cold and clammy. "When's the last time I ever let you down?"

"You haven't . . . yet."

"I never will. You want the bug on ice, you got it. Call me Mr. Pest Control."

"Deliver like you promised me, I'll call you number one in the Miami operation. You blow it, and I'll have to call somebody else."

"I'm on the case."

"Don't let me down. Don't let yourself down."

"Not a chance," Ernesto said. No fucking way.

The line went dead without so much as a goodbye. He was listening to the dial tone as Dolores started rolling him between her palms.

"Bad news?"

"You ask too many questions."

"You're pissed at me for something? I could leave right now if you want me to."

"Who's pissed? Besides, you haven't done your job."

"What job is that?" She was smiling now.

"Keep thinking. It'll come to you."

"I almost had it for a second there. It was on the tip of my tongue."

"Now you're talking."

Magic hands and magic tongue. Ernesto closed his eyes, enjoying the moment and concentrating on Mercado's orders and the implication for himself if he should fail. José was anxious for a tag on La Araña, pushing Ramos, as if he'd been jerking off or something all this time. Mercado had to know it was a risky business going up against the tough kid on the block.

For openers, it had taken six months for him to find out who La Araña was, and when he spelled it out, Mercado nearly shit a cinder block. The tag was next, and so far they were batting zero, even though he'd given it all he had the first time out. It wasn't bad enough he had La Araña's reputation to contend with, plus Costanza's—now he had the late snafu to deal with, dead men out the ass, and anyone he tried to see about the contract now was asking double because of the danger he'd have to face.

No problem.

It was cheap at half the price if he could nail La Araña and make Mercado think he was some kind of superman. Number one in the Miami area was worth the hassle, even if he had to do the job himself.

Well, maybe not.

At last resort perhaps if there was no one dumb enough to take the bait. But this was still Miami, after all—fast money talked and bullshit walked, the way Ernesto understood the game.

La Araña had enjoyed a decent run of luck, but times were changing. The Costanza family had grown too big, too fast, and it was time somebody took them down a peg.

Ernesto Ramos thought he just might be the man to do the job—or supervise at least. From the security of distance, if he had a choice.

There was no point in making any calls tonight. It was too late already, and he needed something for his nerves before he tried again.

Dolores.

"I could use a shower, babe," he said. "You want to scrub my back?"

"I'd rather scrub your front."

"That, too."

17

The mark's apartment was on Harbor Drive, fronting on Bahia Mar. His car was still in place at half past eight, and Gadgets figured he was probably a sluggish riser, staying up till God knows when and sleeping in to compensate.

"We know for sure he's with Mercado?" Blancanales asked.

"Confirmed by Leo, through his touch at the DEA. The Metro boys have pulled him in a couple of times for questioning on homicides, but he's a hands-off kind of guy. Likes delegating the authority and letting someone else go through the door."

"You think he knows enough to make this action worth our time?"

"I'll let it slide if you have a better notion."

"Nope." Politician sipped his cup of coffee. "Just asking."

Schwarz had asked himself the same thing late last night when he'd finished pumping Leo for the name of someone they could lean on. He wasn't thrilled with the resort to an abduction on the street—or in the parking lot, to be precise—but they were getting nowhere with the random hits, uncertain whether they were even tagging the cartels or rousting independents half the time.

This way, if they could sweat the mark for names, at least they had a shot at verifying the assorted targets Lyons had been drawing from Maria Teresina. With a spot of luck they might just get a lead on La Araña and the purpose of their visit to South Florida.

"He's coming."

A year-old mug shot of their mark propped up on the dash confirmed the tentative ID—Ernesto Ramos in the flesh, accompanied by a lady of the type most often seen in taverns after sundown, or in flashy autos headed somewhere else.

"He looks a little tired to me," Schwarz observed.

"I'd chalk it up to too much exercise."

"You figure she's his trainer?"

"Must be. Even a mother couldn't love a face like that."

"He might have other qualities."

"We'll soon find out."

They watched Ramos and the woman say goodbye, a quick peck on the cheek before they split for separate cars. She drove a classic Jaguar and didn't hang around, the gurgle of her twin exhausts already fading by the time Ramos got his key into the ignition of a newish Cadillac—the shrunken kind that looks like every other four-door on the road but costs four times as much.

"You want to take him now?" Pol asked.

"Let's find out where he's going first," Gadgets said. "Could be useful."

"Hey, I'm easy."

"That's what I've heard."

They followed Ramos south on Seabreeze, crossing the Stranahan River on St. Brooks Memorial Causeway into Fort Lauderdale. From there, they picked up Highway 1 and ran due south through Hollywood and Hallandale, past North Miami Beach, until their pigeon caught the Dixie Highway, rolling into North Miami and an office complex on Eighth Avenue.

"Looks like he's taking care of business."

"Either way, let's do it."

Blancanales didn't bother searching for a nearby parking space. They parked in back of him—to cut off his retreat—and both men were EVA before Ramos climbed out of his Cadillac.

"Hey, what—"

Schwarz let him see the silencer-equipped Beretta and nodded toward their car. "We need to have a little talk."

"Aw, shit."

He was about to run, believing he had nothing left to lose, when Blancanales stepped in close and gripped his arm. "It's not a good idea, Ernesto."

"Oh?"

"Fact is, we need you alive. No matter what you do, how many times we have to shoot you in the knees, whatever— that's the bottom line."

"You guys are working for Costanza, right?"

"What makes you think so, Ernie?"

"Hey, my name's Ernesto, man."

"Your name is shit if you don't get into the car right now."

Schwarz emphasized the statement with a motion of his pistol, and Ramos forced a smile. "I thought you needed me alive."

The muzzle drooped another inch or two, sights fixing on the zipper of his slacks.

"We need to hear you sing," Schwarz told him. "Me, I don't care if it's tenor or soprano."

"In the car, you said?"

IT CAME TO LA ARAÑA in a flash that major problems frequently contained their own solution. The latest riddle posed by Miguel had been a puzzler until all the facts were studied.

Costanza's training camp for *los sicarios* had been attacked. The leading suspects were Raul Rodriguez or José Mercado, possibly the two of them acting together, pressing for control of the Colombian narcotics trade. But each had also suffered serious attacks within the past two days. Miguel had said as much without supplying details, which had prompted La Araña to make a few long-distance calls before those details were revealed.

There had been a bank job, where the bandit had burned several million dollars in the vault, dumped millions more in the street, then escaped by helicopter.

At Mercado's nightclub a familiar face—still unidentified—had turned up to ice some bodyguards and set the place on fire. It was an act of provocation, pure and simple, perpetrated by a man who matched the general description of the gunner at Costanza's training camp.

So much for the detective work.

La Araña knew Costanza's leading gunmen—those who could have pulled off such accomplished raids, at any rate—and there were none who fit the profile of the stranger currently at large in Medellín. Luis would never destroy the training camp himself to make his enemies think he had trouble on his hands. And even if he did, for a move like that, he would have spoken to his hitter before he went ahead.

And what was going down in Miami?

Costanza certainly wasn't responsible for recent incidents around Dade County, as La Araña would have been assigned to carry out such raids. The fact that dealers serving the Mercado and Rodriguez families had been earmarked for elimination was apparently designed to point a finger—and it might succeed with strangers, even the authorities—but La Araña couldn't be deceived.

A wild card in the city, then . . . but who?

The hitter smiled. Of course. It was so obvious.

And the solution?

Laughing softly now, La Araña knew exactly what to do—a perfect plan to use the enemy against his own associates, destroy them all, and reinforce the reputation earned with fire and blood. It would be a coup that would confirm La Araña's status as Costanza's strong right arm in the United States, an indispensable associate.

So what if Miguel was waiting in Medellín for a solution to the riddle? Let him wait. He wanted names, a fix upon the enemy, so he could personally take the word back to Luis and receive a pat on the head.

La Araña had no time or patience for the ins and outs of office politics. Results brought lucrative rewards, and there was no good reason why Miguel should share the glory of a job well done in Florida.

Miguel aside, La Araña knew Luis would be waiting for those results. His patience was a limited commodity, and if he thought his hitter was trifling with his business interests—his livelihood—there'd be hell to pay.

Self-confidence aside, La Araña wasn't ready for a face-off with Costanza. One day soon perhaps, but only when the time was right and every preparation had been made. A resolution of the current problem was a step in that direction. Win Costanza's gratitude and take on more authority as the reward, perhaps a bit of a celebration for their common victory.

Luis would never risk a trip to the United States, not while the extradition matter lay before him unresolved. La Araña might go home to Medellín, or they could always meet on neutral ground. A place where both of them could feel secure.

And then . . .

The hitter owed Costanza much in terms of wealth and power, but the past was something best viewed briefly from a distance. Everything Luis could do to make La Araña strong, he'd already done. Aside from the continuing supply of drugs—which anyone could manage once the right connections were secured—he'd outlived his usefulness.

Costanza didn't know it yet, but he was like a dinosaur, already trudging toward extinction, making way for brand-new evolutionary forms.

The master dealer of tomorrow was waiting in the wings, but there was still work to be done before the scepter passed to other hands.

A test of strength and wills was drawing closer, and it would begin tonight. The enemy—or one of them, at any rate—was on his way, a fly about to make contact with La Araña's web.

Once he was tangled in that deadly snare there'd be no escape.

CARL LYONS FOUND a slot three spaces from Maria's car and nosed the rental in, referring to the dashboard digital clock before he shut off the engine.

Ten minutes early.

He could wait.

Maria had reluctantly agreed to let him stand in as her bodyguard that morning, while she made the rounds to look for office space and kept appointments with a couple of security consultants. The assassination of her former security men had prompted their employer to dissolve their standing contract, and her landlord had threatened an eviction notice if the storefront office wouldn't relocate voluntarily. City hall was making sympathetic noises, and donations had increased since the attack, but it was useless if Maria couldn't find a place to rent, or guards to keep the premises secure.

It was an old, familiar game that Lyons had observed before. The terrorists won out, in spite of civic disapproval and disgust, by making their selected target a pariah. If they couldn't kill Maria outright, they would close her office down and strip her of protection, try to drive her out. In time, once she was neutralized, prevented from continuing her drive against the dealers, media attention would evaporate. Life on the streets would settle back to status quo.

But not if Lyons had a say in how the final act went down.

The dealers were already feeling heat from the assorted strikes by Able Team. If Pol and Gadgets bagged their man this morning, if he talked, a new round of assaults would keep the opposition reeling while Maria found another place to put down roots.

If necessary, Lyons was prepared to get in touch with Leo, pull strings with Brognola—anything it took to get Maria settled and back in business for the people of Miami. He was no idealist—certainly no goody-two-shoes—but he recognized the fact that individuals *could* make a difference in the scheme of things.

If no one took a stand and showed the way, then every change was for the worse, a nonstop devolution of the human race, declining into apathy and sloth, with chemicals and twisted fantasies to make it seem that life was still worthwhile. Nobody wanted trouble, but a fighter realized that *someone* had to throw that punch—and maybe take one on the chin—to hold the savages at bay.

For Lyons the decision had been automatic, something he never really had to think about before he acted. Good times came and went, but there was always trouble, always someone looking for an easy touch. They used the law but didn't give a damn about its spirit, or the victims they defiled along the way. When it came down to checking out the bottom line, he knew that force was all the bastards really understood.

His watch said it was time, and Lyons locked the car, moving easily along the concrete walk to reach Maria's flat. From twenty feet away he saw that her door was standing open—just an inch, but far enough—and by the time he reached the threshold, he had the big Colt Python in his hand.

It could be suicide to knock. He stood aside and prodded with a foot to push the door wide open, crouching as he pivoted around the jamb and swept the living room.

The place was trashed, the coffee table and sofa overturned. The cushions had been gutted with a knife, their springs and stuffing on display. Contents of the kitchen cupboards had been scattered on the floor.

"Maria?"

Lyons had no hope she'd answer him, no reason to believe she was still alive, so her voice came out of nowhere, like a hammer stroke between the eyes.

"Back here."

The bedroom.

He took care to check out the kitchen before he made his move—no gunners crouching underneath the breakfast counter—and he kept the closet covered as he inched along the hallway toward Maria's bedroom.

The door was open, but the blinds were drawn, and it was nearly dark inside.

"Maria?"

"Here. Please hurry!"

Lyons fumbled for the light switch, the Python tracking on her voice. The sudden glare revealed her seated on the bed, hands folded in her lap, regarding him with an expression he couldn't define.

"Maria, what—"

Footsteps sounded behind him as he spoke, and Lyons turned to meet them with the Python, knowing as he made the move that he was too late.

The blackjack struck him just above one ear, the impact dropping the Able warrior to his knees. Before he had a chance to fire another roundhouse blow made contact with his shoulder, numbing arm and hand, and the big revolver slipped from his grasp.

He had a glimpse of slacks and a matching jacket as the slugger took a backstep, measuring the kick. Then a size twelve boot exploded in his face. The floor rush up to meet him, and he seemed to plunge right through it, spinning into darkness, falling through the echo of Maria's scream.

"SO HERE'S THE DEAL, Ernesto—if you talk, you walk. Not right away, of course, but once we verify your information, check it out. I guarantee you could do worse."

Ernesto Ramos glared at Blancanales from the chair where he sat handcuffed and shackled. "I'm no fucking stoolie."

"That's right," Schwarz agreed. "You're a fucking pusher, selling poison to children in the street, for all I know. My instinct tells me I should blow your brains out here and now. The thing is, my partner thinks you ought to have a chance to redeem yourself."

"I know this game," Ernesto blustered. "Good cop, bad cop—am I right? Fuck you. I been around."

"Strike one, we're not police," Pol told him, fondling the Beretta as he spoke. "Strike two, there's not a good guy in the house. You want to try for three?"

"Forget it. I can smell a pig from here to Jacksonville. I want my lawyer, man."

"I want to live forever," Blancanales replied. "I guess we've both got disappointments coming."

"Hey, you want to work me over. Be my guest. Won't be the first time, man. I know my rights, and I don't have to say a fucking word."

Schwarz glanced at Blancanales, then shrugged. "The guy knows his rights. I guess we're screwed."

"I guess."

Ernesto cracked a wicked smile. "Damn right, you're screwed. My lawyer's going to sue your ass for every dime you got."

"You want to do it, or should I?"

Schwarz drew his pistol and cocked it. "It's my turn, man. You did the last one."

"Hey, do what?"

"Turns out you're worthless, Ernie." Blancanales lifted the Beretta and aimed at the startled face. "Bye-bye."

"Hold on a minute, will you? We can make a deal, for Christ's sake."

"How? You know your rights, remember?"

"Fuck my rights, okay? Just ask your questions and let's get this over with."

Pol glanced at Schwarz. "I think he's full of it. If you want to do it, go ahead."

"My pleasure."

"Wait!"

"Why should I?"

"You want information, right? I've got it, anything you want to know. If I have to, I can make some calls and find out more, okay?"

"Let's start with something easy. Who's your boss?"

"Well,—"

"I knew it," Blancanales snapped. "Go on and waste this piece of garbage."

"Mercado, dammit! Are you satisfied? This kind of talk can get me killed."

"Life's hard. You know about the hits in town last night?"

"Who doesn't?"

"We're concerned about affiliations, Ernie. Who owns who?"

"The guys who got blown up, you mean?"

"That's what I mean."

"One of them worked with me, and the others all did business with Raul Rodriguez."

"The Costanza people?"

"High and dry. If you ask me, they were pulling off the hits."

"One more, for all the marbles."

"Yeah?"

"A name."

"Am I supposed to guess, or what?"

"We're looking for the Spider. La Araña."

Ernesto Ramos seemed to mean it this time when he smiled. "You don't want much."

"Enough for you to live on maybe. Or to die for."

"I was working on that name for six months, but what the hell. If you want to take it off my hands, I'm not complaining."

"Well?"

"It's funny when you think about it. All that time I'm looking for a macho man to pin the tail on, and I never had a clue La Araña was a broad."

"Let's hear the punch line," Blancanales snapped.

"Maria Teresina, man. The same bitch who wants to clean up Miami. Is that a laugh, or what?"

18

The airstrip north of Medellín was dubbed "Miami International" in jest because so many flights departed from its runway bound for southern Florida. On any given day as many as two dozen planes took off or landed, some of them staying overnight as pilots closed their deals with brokers, waiting on their cargos of *la merca*. Only La Guajira's airfields saw more action in the cocaine trade, and Bolan had decided it was time to give Miami International a rest.

Grimaldi drove, as usual, but this time Bolan rode the shot gun seat, their vehicle a rugged four-wheel-drive with guts enough to leave the road behind if necessary in a pinch. It wasn't flying, but the pilot didn't seem to mind. "We're bound to piss some people off, you know?"

"I'm counting on it," Bolan said. "Costanza owns the strip. He's got a shake-up coming after the surprise we gave Mercado and Rodriguez."

"I thought it would have hit the fan by now."

"They're playing safe. With three billion dollars on the table, you don't want to scrub the game unless you see you've got no choice."

"I guess."

"It's coming," Bolan promised him. "With Able turning up the heat around Miami, Phoenix on their case in Panama, they're bound to crack before too long."

"If it was me," Grimaldi said, "I think I'd take myself a nice vacation. Somewhere in the Himalayas if they've got a Howard Johnson's."

"These guys don't know how to run away. You've seen the way they rag their government on extradition. Even when they're hiding out, they can't leave well enough alone."

"You figure this should be the final straw?"

"I gave up telling fortunes, Jack. Whichever way it goes, we have to keep the pressure on till something breaks."

"Suppose it's us?"

"That's why we're getting such terrific pay."

"Oh, yeah. I knew there had to be a reason."

On Bolan's order Jack pulled off the road a mile before they reached the airstrip, dropping into four-wheel low as he negotiated mud and twisted roots to hide the vehicle some fifty feet inside the forest. When he had the Rover turned around and ready for a swift departure, both men skinned off their civvies and suited up in camouflage fatigues. In turn, they dipped their fingers into jars of war paint, daubing streaks of green and gray across their hands and faces.

Both men were packing CAR-15s, a compact version of the classic M-16 with shorter barrel and a telescoping stock. They carried bandoliers of extra magazines, plus fragmentation and chemical grenades. Grimaldi's side arm was his favorite Beretta, worn in military leather on his hip. Bolan doubled up on handguns, wearing the Beretta 93-R in an armpit rig and the mighty Desert Eagle Magnum autoloader on his belt. Assorted knives, garrotes, and other bits of martial gear were tucked away in sheaths and pockets, where the warriors could lay hands on them at need.

Bolan checked his compass, pointing through the trees where sunlight filtered through the canopy of leaves. "I make it half a mile in that direction, north-northwest."

"Sounds fair."

They made the trek in silence, more or less, which meant they had to take their time. A man who told you it was possible to travel quietly *and* quickly in a forest where the undergrowth hadn't been cleared for generations was a liar or fool. A narrow game trail helped, but they were still required to check out every step—for trip wires and assorted other booby traps, as well as snakes or quicksand, fallen branches that would snap beneath their weight and pinpoint their position for the enemy.

It took the best part of an hour to cover half a mile, and Bolan knew it had to be getting on Grimaldi's nerves. The pilot was accustomed to a different kind of warfare, swooping from the sky at dizzy speeds to blast and strafe his enemies, or dueling with them in the air. It was a different world below, where mud became the standard medium and killing was a face-to-face experience.

The forest had been cleared a hundred yards or so ahead of them from east to west. They huddled at the tree line, checking out the fuel tanks, hangars and garage, four airplanes parked and waiting near the strip. On Bolan's right, some sixty yards away, a feeder road connected with the highway back to Medellín, and there were sentries lounging on the grass with automatic weapons, covering the obvious approach.

He started counting heads, saw five men visible, and estimated there had to be several other men inside the makeshift office and the hangars on his left. They'd assume the unseen, anyway, to play it safe.

"Your call."

Grimaldi shrugged. "Left, I guess."

"Three minutes for position and then we move. Okay?"

"No sweat."

Grimaldi faded back and started following the tree line westward, angling for a point directly opposite the fuel tanks. Bolan watched him for a moment, then turned away and headed in the opposite direction toward the access road and prefab office.

There was no way in the world two men could surround an airstrip, even one this size, but they could raise some hell and take advantage of surprise to carry off the play.

Surprise, and maybe luck.

Considering the circumstances, the Executioner knew he had more or less exhausted strategy, per se. From this point on they'd be playing it by ear.

A funeral march for some, perhaps for all concerned.

Refusing to accept the prospect of defeat, he put the morbid thought away and concentrated on the next two minutes while he still had time to plan ahead.

Before it hit the fan.

"You LOOK LIKE HELL."

McCarter tried to smile at Calvin James, but gave it up. It simply wasn't worth the effort.

"Funny, that's exactly how I feel."

"What happened to the meeting?" Katz asked, arriving at McCarter's bedside with a mug of coffee steaming in each hand.

"I haven't got a clue," the Briton replied, ignoring angry protests from his ribs and elsewhere as he sat upright and took one of the mugs from Katz. "One minute we were wrapping up our business, then a goon squad crashed the party and it went to hell."

"No warning?"

"Arevalo wasn't into lookouts. I suppose he didn't know who he could trust."

"About the evidence..."

"He wasn't joking. Glossy black-and-whites. Caseros with Costanza's man, Ortega, and José Mercado—snapped at different times, of course."

"A doubleheader," James remarked.

"Plus two more photos of a room supposedly inside the presidential mansion. Lots of gear laid out in preparation for a Santeria ritual."

Encizo cursed and shifted closer to the bed. "You're saying that Caseros is a *brujo?*"

"I'm not saying anything. The captain laid it out that way, and now he's dead. As far as I can see, we're chasing shadows on the voodoo end."

"Perhaps. But if Caseros *is* involved—"

"We need to concentrate on something we can use," Katz interrupted.

"Costanza and Mercado?" Manning asked.

"It would be interesting to know if either one of them has made Caseros dealing with the enemy."

"Fat chance," McCarter said, "without the photographs."

"You saw the negatives?"

He shook his head. "If Arevalo had them with him, they weren't inside the envelope."

"We've got a chance, then."

"Slim to none, I'd say."

"The captain might have passed on lookouts, but he wasn't working solo, either. Someone had to take the photographs, develop them and pass them on."

"The voodoo shots were from someone at the house, a member of the staff. I wasn't offered any names. The rest were taken at an airport and a bungalow, presumably somewhere inside the city. Tracing the photographer could take a bloody lifetime, and we've barely got a week."

"It's something we can shoot for, anyway."

McCarter changed the subject, meeting Katz's gaze. "What happened with your friend?"

"Acquaintance," Katz corrected. "We spoke, but that's about the size of it. He's bitter over being flushed out of Mossad. Somebody else's fault, of course. A patriot abused—you know the kind of thing I mean."

"A major dose of sour grapes," James offered.

"Worse. The ego's only part of it. He honestly believes the politicians set him up, some kind of human sacrifice to pacify the media."

"And did they?" Manning asked.

"What difference does it make? He's training killers for the drug cartels. I don't care what he's been through. Someone has to stop him. Now."

"You didn't scare him off by any chance?" McCarter asked.

"He doesn't scare." Katz paused to light a cigarette before continuing. "I don't mean that he'll sit around and wait for us to take him out, by any means, but Isaac knows the ropes. He won't be easy."

"Shit," James said, "who is?"

"Caseros maybe, if we found a way to turn Costanza's family and the other big cartels against him."

"With the photographs?" McCarter took no pains to hide his personal disgust. "They're gone, all right? I blew it, plain and simple."

"Maybe not. The link to Arevalo came from the CIA and State through Stony Man. I doubt they'd stake their hopes on one young officer, regardless of his rank."

"So what?"

"So maybe they have other contacts we can tap. Somebody close enough to know about the photographs and furnish copies, maybe even lead us to the negatives."

"With Arevalo dead don't count on volunteers."

"That goes both ways. Some of the dissidents will run for cover, certainly. I'm counting on a few of them to realize they could be next unless they dump Caseros soon."

"It's worth a shot," James said.

"Right now it's all we have."

"And while we wait?" McCarter asked. "What next?"

"You said a member of the house staff took the voodoo shots?"

"Supposedly. A bodyguard, I think he said. The photographs were taken with Caseros out of town."

"All right," Katz said, "we're looking for a presidential bodyguard who hangs around to mind the store while others are away."

"You think Caseros takes the same crew with him every time?"

"It's something we can check at least."

"Okay, agreed."

"But first," the gruff Israeli told McCarter, "you need rest."

"I'm fine."

"If so, then you'll be even better when you've had some sleep. No arguments. Right now I wouldn't trust you on my blind side. We need time to get you sorted out and make sure nothing's banged up inside."

"You're lucky we weren't any later," James informed McCarter. "The way I hear it, you were all set up to be the guest of honor at a wienie roast."

"I think you'll find that I can rise to the occasion."

"Guess we'll have to find that out another time, old son."

"Rest now," Katz said, interrupting their good-natured banter. "If you like, you can consider it an order."

Scowling as the other members of the team filed out, McCarter let himself relax a bit when they were gone. He did need a rest, of course—and even that wouldn't eliminate the pain entirely—but he didn't plan to miss the final showdown with Caseros and his goons.

If Katz expected him to watch the action from the sidelines, he was in for a surprise. No order from on high would keep McCarter off the firing line when it was payback time.

GRIMALDI CROUCHED behind a waist-high wall of ferns and scanned the runway right and left before he checked his watch. Another forty seconds until blast-off, and he had the fuel tanks lined up on his right, some thirty yards away. Across the strip the hangars faced directly toward his hiding place, with the garage and office building partially obscured.

That end of it was Bolan's, anyway, but Jack knew trouble could arrive from any corner of the killing ground once they began. Five men were in view, and as he watched, one of them disappeared inside the nearest hangar, swallowed by the shadows there.

Ten seconds.

Lining up the shot, Grimaldi started counting down the doomsday numbers in his mind. As "zero" came and went, he stroked the trigger of his CAR-15, not waiting for the sound of Bolan's fire to put the ball in play.

After a short, precision burst, Grimaldi lifted off the trigger and *did* hear the big guy firing from the far end of the strip. In front of him he saw the jets of airplane fuel erupt from half a dozen holes, the sharp high-octane fumes enough to clear the sinuses as gas began to puddle on the ground.

He palmed a frag grenade and yanked the safety pin, an easy underhand sufficient for his needs. Facedown before the blast sent shock waves rippling across the grass, he didn't see the tanks erupt in leaping flames. But he was on his feet and moving shortly after the first one blew apart, providing friend and foe alike with a convincing glimpse of hell on earth.

The rolling smoke cloud covered him as he zigzagged across the runway, dodging toward the hangars. In the nearest open door a short guy with a submachine gun saw him coming and squeezed off a burst that missed Grimaldi by at least ten feet.

He answered on the run, another miss, but his was close enough to force the gunner back inside. A shotgun roared downrange, and Grimaldi could hear the buckshot pellets pattering around him, mixed with smoking bits of shrapnel as the second tank went off.

The Stony Man flyboy hosed a burst in the direction of the gun's report, no target visible, and kept on running, holding to his course. He was within a dozen strides of touchdown when the short guy rose from cover, spraying automatic fire across his track.

Grimaldi hit the turf, the CAR-15 on-line and tracking for a target. The short guy fired from the hip like Rambo Junior, wasting most of it as Grimaldi squeezed off a 3-round burst that laid him on his back.

One down, and Grimaldi was on the move before his cartridge casings settled on the grass. He reached the open hangar door and lobbed a frag grenade inside, retreating toward the building next in line before it blew.

He never knew what set the hangar off exactly—a stash of extra fuel inside, a plane with shrapnel-ruptured tanks—but he was close enough to feel the heat when flames shot through the open doorway, followed by a solid secondary blast. A portion of the tin roof lifted off, the east wall buckling from concussion and the sudden heat.

Grimaldi let the shock wave carry him along, propelling him in the direction of the second hangar. On the strip two men were running toward him, both with pistols in their hands, and he unloaded with the CAR-15, his last rounds dropping both men in their tracks. One of them wasn't finished yet, his weapon spitting at Grimaldi, forcing the pilot to duck behind the hangar as he fed his piece a brand-new magazine.

Pinned down . . . or was he?

Fading back along the hangar's western wall, Grimaldi found another door in back, half-open. He was edging closer, covering the doorway, when a tall man lurched across the threshold, leveling a shotgun at Grimaldi's chest.

The guns went off together, and Grimaldi had a glimpse of his assailant reeling, going down, before a giant fist struck home above his heart and drove him to the ground.

THE EXECUTIONER WAS ready when Grimaldi blew the fuel tanks, lining up his shot and squeezing off a figure eight that nailed the sentries before they had a chance to break from their position on the road. He caught a glimpse of movement near the hangars, gunmen tracking on Grimaldi as the pilot made his run, but Bolan had his own objectives, sprinting out from cover toward the plywood office building and the small garage.

The sound of gunfire and explosions brought two men out on the office steps, one of them juggling a pistol in his hand, the other seemingly unarmed. The gunner saw death coming from the corner of his eye, and turned to pump a reckless round at the warrior from a range of forty yards. It would have been a miracle if he had scored the first time out, and Bolan heard the bullet pass him by at least three feet away.

He answered with a running burst that drove the shooter back against the doorjamb, squeezing off another wild round toward the sky. The unarmed man stood gaping for an instant, turning toward the open door with cover on his mind. Bolan helped him get there with a 3-round burst between the shoulder blades.

There would be no civilians at "Miami International," and whether any given dealer had a gun in hand was totally beside the point. Between them, with their poison shipments headed north, the poison pushers were responsible for countless deaths already, from Miami and New Orleans to Seattle and L.A. They had no mercy coming, and the Executioner didn't feel generous.

He stepped across the prostrate body, probing with the CAR-15 before he moved inside the office to discover army surplus furniture—a desk and several chairs, a stubby filing cabinet—and nothing else. There might be information he could use inside the files, but the warrior didn't have the time to sort it out. Instead, he yanked the top drawer open, primed a thermite canister and dropped it inside. Retreating in a rush, he had an extra heartbeat left before the white-hot coals began to eat their way through paper, steel and plywood, setting off a blaze that licked at Bolan's heels.

Before the Executioner reached the cinder-block garage a wounded gunner opened up on him from the middle of the runway, staggering and firing on the move. He lost his footing as he ran and stumbled into Bolan's line of fire, a string of 5.56 mm tumblers spinning him around and dropping him before he had a chance to find his range.

Still moving, the warrior palmed a frag grenade and lobbed it toward the line of aircraft waiting on the border of the strip, its detonation shearing off the wing of one small craft and punching shrapnel through a second fuselage. He sprayed the next two planes in line with automatic fire and saw flames spreading to consume all four as he slid into cover, shoulders pressed against the eastern wall of the garage.

There was no sign of Jack Grimaldi in the drifting clouds of smoke.

He fed the CAR-15 another magazine and jacked a round into the firing chamber as he edged around the wall to check inside the small garage. The door was standing open, and he shouldered through it in a rolling entry, covering the dark interior, alert for any sign of movement that would mark an enemy.

Oil drums lined one wall, and a workbench on the other was strewn with tools. A motor-driven winch was standing in the middle of the room, an airplane's engine block suspended in a sling composed of oily chains.

A sound of scuffling footsteps brought him to his knees, his weapon leveled at the doorway. He was ready for the kill when Jack Grimaldi showed himself, his camou tunic shredded in the front, the Kevlar vest beneath it marked by powder burns.

"You ought to see the other guy," Grimaldi remarked.

"No thanks."

"We finished here?"

"Looks like. Are you okay?"

"I feel like someone dropped a Buick on my ribs, but I'm still breathing, so I guess that's an affirmative."

"We'll get someone to check you out back in town."

"I'll let you know."

The Executioner stood and set the safety on his CAR-15. "You want to help me light this up?"

"I wouldn't miss it for the world."

They tossed two thermite cans—one on the workbench, one among the oil drums—and retreated toward the runway as the chemicals caught fire. In time they'd reduce the cinder blocks to cinders, and the only trace remaining of "Miami International" would be its runway, littered with debris and bodies.

"I'm getting too damn old for this," Grimaldi complained as they approached the shelter of the trees.

"Says who?"

"My ass. The way it's dragging, I believe I may have left it back there on the strip."

"I would've noticed."

"That makes one of us. A little ride, you said."

"Round trip," the warrior said. "I can't complain."

"I wonder if Costanza's going to feel the same?"

"Fair's fair. I guess we ought to ask."

"You're kidding, right?"

Bolan shook his head.

"I was afraid of that."

19

Luis Costanza was sitting down to breakfast when the telephone began to ring. Despite a brief, involuntary tremor in his hands, he forced himself to ignore the instrument, refusing to be shaken by the prospect of another crisis, more bad news.

It had been nearly three o'clock before he'd drifted into fitful sleep, the last call from Ortega playing through his mind before the pills had kicked in and darkness had overcome his racing thought. At that, there had been no escape from nightmares, twisted faces leering at him from the shadows of his own subconscious, challenging Costanza to a contest, goading him to prove himself.

According to Ortega, Raul Rodriguez had been putting feelers out to fix a meeting, somewhere safe on neutral ground, where both Rodriguez and Mercado would deliver proof they weren't involved in the attack on his training camp. Costanza, in his turn, would be permitted—he, *permitted*, like a common peasant!—to persuade them of his innocence in certain raids on their respective organizations.

The call had come as a surprise, although Costanza had expected something of the sort. Rodriguez and Mercado were a pair of crafty bastards, as slippery as garden slugs and equally repugnant to the touch. Their arrogance was legendary, and Costanza wouldn't put it past them to attempt a double cross. In fact, he would expect no less.

And yet . . .

He still couldn't explain the raids his two competitors had suffered. Clearly they suspected him, as he suspected them of razing his academy. But a preliminary meeting might help clear the air, if nothing else. Another player in the game meant danger for them all, and if it came to open warfare in the streets, Costanza might want temporary allies on his side.

He had begun to peel the hard-boiled egg, meticulously working on the shell to pick it clean, when he was conscious of a presence at his elbow. The houseman frowned apologetically and offered him the telephone, its long extension cord strung out behind him like a tail.

"Who is it?"

"I don't know, sir. He says he has important news. I don't know what to tell him, but he says you have to know."

Costanza cursed beneath his breath and accepted the receiver. "Yes?"

He didn't recognize the voice that said in English, "It's too bad about your airstrip, guy."

"There must be some mistake," Costanza answered, but he felt the worm of dread begin to wriggle in his gut.

"You made it. Somebody wants you out of business in a hurry. You've been stepping on the wrong damn toes."

"Who is this?"

"We haven't met, but I'll be looking forward to it. Maybe one day soon."

"The airstrip?"

"Closed for renovation, you might say. Of course, you'll need another crew. The boys you've got, well, when I was out there, they were sleeping on the job. I couldn't wake them, no matter how hard I tried."

Costanza clutched the phone so tightly that his knuckles turned white, but when he spoke again his voice was in control. "You've been in touch with me before, I think."

"You're thinking right. I wouldn't be surprised if we're in touch again."

"And your employer?"

"Like I told you, somebody who thinks you've hogged the show too long."

"You've cost me money, but I still admire your style," Costanza said, surprised to realize it was true to some extent. "I'd like to meet you face-to-face."

"I bet you would." The caller's tone was vaguely mocking. "Thing is, I might have to drop in by surprise."

"A man of your abilities, whatever you're receiving now, I'll double it."

"No sale."

"Integrity? Another quality to be admired. All right, let's say three times your present salary."

"It's not the money, guy. The thing is, I like working for the winning side."

"And you expect I'll lose?" Costanza didn't know if he should scream or laugh out loud.

"It's in the cards."

"In that case we have nothing more to say."

"Not yet."

Costanza eased the telephone receiver down, conscious of his adversary on the other end, still listening, alert to any sign of rage or other weakness. Silence was all the victory he could manage at the moment, but he pulled it off.

The houseman hurried over as Costanza snapped his fingers, reading his employer's face and standing clear in case of an explosion. What he got instead were tones Costanza might have used in church.

"I want Ortega on the line within the next two minutes. Also, double the guards around the house. If anyone approaches closer than a hundred meters, I want that person secured and brought to me."

"If there's resistance?"

Costanza forced a smile. "I didn't say they had to be alive."

He'd confirm the airstrip raid before he made another move, and if the call was accurate—as he believed—it would require some measure of response.

The problem was, Costanza didn't know whom he should punish . . . yet.

But it was coming.

He could feel it in his bones.

COSTANZA HAD IMPRESSED the Executioner with his control. The guy was not a screamer—on the telephone at least—and Bolan was prepared to bet that icy nerves supported every move Costanza made. Unlike some adversaries he'd faced, the dealer wasn't likely to unravel or to explode and blow his game. He seemed the kind of fighter who would hang on until the final shot was fired, and go down in defeat—if he want down at all—demanding one more chance to prove himself.

The others . . .

It was enough, for openers, to plant the seeds of doubt between competitors and let them take on one another, but sitting back and watching the cartels indulge in a flagrant bloodbath hardly qualified as strategy. If something didn't break by noon the next day, Bolan would be forced to reassess the plan and seek another angle of attack.

The safehouse was a small suburban bungalow that rented by the month, arranged by Leo Turrin through his contacts in the DEA. It was a toss-up whether any of the major dealers knew about the place, but Bolan wasn't sleeping there. In fact, its only points of interest were the telephone and a sophisticated answering machine that occupied a counter near the kitchen sink. Remote control meant Bolan didn't have to pass within a hundred miles of the address to claim his messages, as long as he had access to another phone.

He chose a public booth downtown and dialed the number of the safehouse, palming the remote-control device as the telephone began to ring. A nondescript recorded voice came on with brief instructions, first in Spanish, then repeating them in English, and on cue he pressed the plastic box against the mouthpiece of his handset, thumbing back a switch to send a sonic tone along the wires.

He waited for the automated voice to say, "You have one message," followed by another tone, some clicking on the line, and then a voice he recognized.

"Hey, Striker, this is L.J. Call me when you get a chance."

L.J.—for Leonard Justice—was the working alias employed by Leo Turrin in his role as Hal Brognola's number two. Whatever news he might be passing on, the Executioner was certain Leo wouldn't waste a call over trivia.

He used the credit card again, but this time dialed direct to Leo's private line in Wonderland. The same familiar voice responded after half a dozen rings.

"Hello?"

"I got a call from Mr. Justice on my answering machine. Is he around, by any chance?"

"I'm sorry. He's not in right now. Was there a message?"

"Never mind. I'll call back."

The line went dead, and Bolan started counting down the minutes, knowing it would take a minimum of ten for Leo to evacuate his office, ride the elevator down and walk a block to reach a corner deli where one of the pay phones was labeled with a sign that made it permanently Out of Order. The proprietor got twenty bucks a week to keep the sign in place and look the other way when strangers dropped in unexpectedly to take a call in the "inoperative" booth. It didn't happen often, maybe twice a month on average, and it pleased the deli owner to reflect in private on his "undercover work."

Twelve minutes later he punched the second number up direct and was rewarded with an instant answer on the other end.

"Joe's Pizza."

"You deliver?"

Leo chuckled. "I'm afraid you're not within our normal servicing area."

"My luck. Why don't you read the menu to me, anyway?"

"Sounds fair. I heard you had an interest in the Phoenix special.".

"That's affirmative. The last I heard, there was a question about how much of the product was in stock."

"We're back in business," Leo told him. "It was touch and go, I understand, but everything's on track."

"Results?"

"No confirmation yet. The rabbi thinks another day or two at least."

"Miami?"

Leo hesitated. "We've been advertising there," he said, "but there's a problem with the Spider-Man concession. No hard details, but we'll have to iron it out before we're done."

"I see."

Between the lines it meant that Able team had hit a snag in the pursuit of La Araña. Someone, Pol or Gadgets, had reported danger to Ironman—Lyons—but they hadn't taken time to spell it out, or else . . .

He pushed the grim alternative away and concentrated on the job at hand as Leo's voice distracted him. "You're hanging in, I guess?"

"I've made preliminary contact with the competition," Bolan reported, "but it's too early to predict which way they'll go. A price war wouldn't hurt us, but they might hang tough."

"Just so they hang."

"You read my mind. Are we still looking at that deadline for the job?"

"'Fraid so. I'd like to give you all the time you need, but as it is, we're on the clock."

"You'll keep me posted?"

"That's affirmative. You do the same."

The plan allowed Costanza and his opposition one more day to make a move, whichever way it went. The Executioner had done his best to drive a wedge between them, and he was prepared to reassess the game if they came out with a united front. Meanwhile he had an afternoon to kill in Medellín, and he was looking forward to a momentary break from hit-and-run. The battle would be joined again before he had a chance to make himself at home, but he could still unwind a bit, stand down from red alert and watch the home team from a "safe" position on the sidelines.

Soon there'd be no safe place for any of the major narcobarons in Medellín. A cleansing fire was on the way, and none who stood before its heat would walk away unscathed.

Sometimes, he knew, the only way to rid a rat-infested house of vermin was to burn it down.

A few more hours, counting down, and Bolan meant to strike himself a match.

"HE DIDN'T ASK about the White House," Leo said, "but something tells me he wouldn't care right now."

"That's one," Brognola answered, scowling. "I know some folks on Pennsylvania Avenue who might not be amused."

"We've run things down before without approval from the top." Even as he said it, Leo knew it sounded lame.

"We haven't done a job like this since the McNerney operation in Honduras, and the Man was watching that one all the way." Brognola frowned, expelling smoke. "I think it's time for you to think about deniability."

"Like hell."

"I mean it, Leo. This could still go either way, but I don't like the feel. It's shaky in Miami, and we're getting nowhere fast in Panama. As good as Striker is, the odds might be too long this time. No reason why you should bite the bullet when it comes out that I exceeded my authority."

"I volunteered, remember?"

"And I'm giving you the opportunity to change your mind."

"No thanks."

"Goddamn it, Leo—"

"Save your breath. I'm in, okay? Whichever way it goes, I'm not prepared to call it a mistake."

"You had your chance."

"That's right."

"Okay, in that case, how'd you like to get some sun?"

"Miami?"

"I'm not satisfied the way it's shaking out down there. We've still got problems with the DEA and Metro-Dade as far as leaks. I need a lookout I can trust."

"I'm out of here."

"A day or two, that's all."

"Whatever."

"Right. Whatever."

As he moved toward the elevator, Turrin felt a sudden rush he hadn't experienced in months—or was it years? The desk in Wonderland was nice and safe, all things considered, but the plain fact was, he missed the action now and then.

Like now, for instance.

"Save me some," he muttered as the elevator took him down. "I'm on my way."

"THERE'S STILL no answer," Blancanales said as he returned and settled in the shotgun seat.

"God*damn* it!"

"Southwest Twenty-fourth, he said?"

"That's it."

Schwarz put the car in motion, rolling south toward the apartment where they hoped to find Maria Teresina—alias La Araña—waiting for them in the center of her web.

"He could be working something on his own," Politician offered, sounding doubtful.

"Right. Without a call?"

"It wouldn't be the first time."

"He was seeing her last night, and now he isn't in his room. If you ask me, they either spent the night together or they're out somewhere."

Schwarz didn't voice the third alternative—the possibility that La Araña had already seen through Lyons and arranged a trap. He didn't want to think about Ironman lying in an alley somewhere with a bullet in his head, or doubled up inside an oil drum, floating in the bay.

"You figure she was using him to roust the competition all along?"

"I don't know what was in her mind," Schwarz said, "but that's the way it plays. Unless Ernesto's got an Oscar coming, we've been working on Mercado and Rodriguez while Costanza takes a snooze.''

"Carl wouldn't let it slip."

"He wouldn't have to. One and one still adds up to two, okay? She gives him names, addresses, and the guys get hit. He figured she was bound to scope it out in another day or two."

"Suppose he's with her?" Blancanales asked.

"Depends. If we have time to talk, there shouldn't be a problem. Otherwise..."

Schwarz knew he didn't have to finish it. Their mission in Miami was to find and crush La Araña, thereby crippling Costanza's distribution network long enough for Bolan and the men of Phoenix Force to try to work a miracle down south. If they were able to disrupt Rodriguez and Mercado at the same time, fine, but neither of Costanza's two competitors had been their first priority.

And when they found La Araña, they'd finish it. No prisoners and no appeals. The DEA and Metro-Dade had tried and failed with the conventional approach, and it was time to play for keeps—one problem being how Ironman would react . . . if he was still alive.

Lyons should have been in touch that morning, one way or another, and it made no difference where he spent the night. In all their time together, working out of Stony Man, he'd displayed no sign of bashfulness, and Gadgets couldn't see him starting now.

A failure to communicate meant something had detained him, and the word from their informant, fingering Maria Teresina, narrowed down the possibilities in Schwarz's mind. For instance, it was safe to say that Lyons hadn't been kidnapped by a UFO, nor had he simply overslept, forgetting that he was supposed to touch base with his teammates every morning rain or shine. He *might* be shacking up, but even iron men took a breather sometime, and it didn't take much strength to dial a telephone.

The options were distressing, and they all spelled trouble, with Maria Teresina looming large in each and every one of the scenarios. No matter how Schwarz tried to turn it all around and see another angle, there she was—the Spider, crouching over Lyons, poised to strike.

"What was the number?" Blancanales asked.

Schwarz played it back from memory, examining the line of cars as he performed a circuit of the parking lot on Twenty-fourth.

"Right there."

It was the rental Lyons drove, an empty space beside it. Gadgets nosed his own car in and turned the engine off.

"It's going to piss him off if we crash the party," Blancanales said.

"Too bad. If he wanted privacy, he should have dropped a coin."

He reached inside his jacket, drawing the Beretta, and retrieved its silencer from underneath the driver's seat. Another moment and the bulky tube was threaded into place. Blancanales checked his Ingram's load and flicked off the safety.

"No matter what," Schwarz added.

Pol looked at him and nodded solemnly. "No matter what."

They locked the car and left it, moving two abreast along the walk, their weapons close at hand but out of sight. Schwarz counted off the numbered doors, backtracking once when they got lost, and finally they stood before Maria Teresina's flat.

"Let's be polite," Pol suggested.

"It couldn't hurt."

Gadgets pressed the bell and felt the door begin to swing away from him. Unlocked. Not even closed.

"Hello?"

He followed the Beretta through and stepped aside to give Pol room, already scoping out the disarray inside. Someone had trashed the place—not carefully, but with a vengeance. Gadgets wondered how the neighbors could have missed it, finally deciding they were probably afraid to get involved.

"Nice place," Pol said.

"It was."

"Is anybody here?"

No answer came from the corridor that had to have a bedroom at the other end. They checked it out. More disarray, the signs of a determined, hasty search.

"What's this?" Schwarz knelt to take a closer look, but he already knew. Two steps inside the bedroom there were rusty-colored splotches on the carpet.

Blood.

A great deal more was pooled near the bed.

Schwarz stood and stepped around the splatter, drawing back the tangled bedding to reveal a pair of naked bloody shoulders, ragged veins and sinew where the head and neck should be. "Oh, shit."

He drew the blankets back, revulsion vying with relief as he discovered that the corpse was female. There was no mistake on that score, even with the head and hands and feet hacked off.

"You think?" Pol said.

He shrugged and dropped the blood-soaked blankets back across the ruin of a human being. "Don't ask me. I never saw the lady. Not like that at least."

"One thing."

"I hear you."

Only there were *two* things nagging at his mind.

If this pathetic piece of meat was La Araña, who had done the job?

And where the hell was Lyons, either way?

———————————

The heart-stopping action continues in the second book of The Medellín Trilogy: Evil Kingdom, *coming in June.*

AGENTS

The action-packed new series of the DEA.... Sudden death is a way of life at the drug-enforcement administration—in an endless full-frontal assault on America's toughest war: drugs. For Miami-based maverick Jack Fowler, it's a war he'll fight to the end.

TRIGGER PULL

PAUL MALONE

In TRIGGER PULL, a narc's murder puts Fowler on a one-man vengeance trail of Miami cops on the take and a Bahamian king-pin. Stalked by Colombian gunmen and a hit team of Metro-Dade's finest, Fowler brings the players together in a win-or-lose game where survival depends on the pull of a trigger.

The Executioner's battle against South American drug lords rages on in Book II of The Medellín Trilogy.

THE EXECUTIONER EVIL KINGDOM

The odds of winning are getting slimmer by the minute as the situation heats up. PHOENIX FORCE is trapped in a surprise invasion, one of ABLE TEAM's members is missing, and THE EXECUTIONER is moving in on Colombia's reigning drug czar.

For this powder keg of action, be sure to get your copy of EVIL KINGDOM!

Available in June at your favorite retail outlet, or order your copy now:

THE MEDELLÍN TRILOGY

BOOK I : Blood Rules (THE EXECUTIONER #149)	$3.50 ☐
BOOK II : Evil Kingdom (352-page MACK BOLAN)	$4.50 ☐
BOOK III: Message to Medellín (THE EXECUTIONER #151)	$3.50 ☐
Total Amount	_____
Plus 75¢ postage ($1.00 in Canada)	_____
Total Payable	_____

Please send a check or money order payable to Gold Eagle Books:

In the U.S.
Gold Eagle Books
3010 Walden Ave.
P.O. Box 1325,
Buffalo, NY 14269-1325

In Canada
Gold Eagle Books
P.O. Box 609,
Fort Erie, Ontario
L2A 5X3

Canadian residents add applicable federal and provincial taxes.

Please Print:

Name: _____

Address: _____

City: _____

State/Prov.: _____

Zip/Postal Code: _____

SB23-1

WELCOME TO THE FUTURE—
A FUTURE THAT WELCOMES NO ONE

SURVIVAL 2000

RENEGADE WAR
James McPhee

David Rand's brutal lessons in survival continue in the second book of Gold Eagle's riveting SURVIVAL 2000 series.

Amid a chilling landscape of fiery skies and frozen ground, Rand searches for his kidnapped family, learning to hunt, steal and kill in order to survive in this nightmarish world of the future.

Don't miss this gripping look at the struggle for survival in a future mercilessly altered by destruction.

GOLD EAGLE

**The Eagle now lands at different times
at your retail outlet!**

Be sure to look for your favorite action adventure from Gold Eagle on these dates each month.

Publication Month	In-Store Dates
May	April 24
June	May 22
July	June 19
August	July 24

We hope that this new schedule will be convenient for you.

Please note: There may be slight variations in on-sale dates in your area due to differences in shipping and handling. GEDATES-R